"I need a fiancé and I need one now!"

This was worse than Justin had thought. "I'm sorry, but there's no way Ross is leaving the hospital anytime soon."

"Then what about you?" Hayley clutched his arm in a death grip.

"Me?" Justin was floored. "I'm not an actor!"

"You don't have to *act*. You have to be Sloane Devereaux, my fiancé." Suddenly noticing her painful grip on his arm, she released him and took a step back. "Listen, my mother and sisters are over by the fountain. They're expecting to meet my fiancé and go to the wedding rehearsal. The limousine is waiting. *Please*."

Justin knew desperation when he saw it. "I've never done anything like this before." He exhaled. "What do I do?"

Hayley glanced toward the fountain. Her family, tired of waiting for an introduction, had decided to greet their prospective in-law themselves. Panicked, Hayley turned to Justin. "Quick!" She flung her arms around his neck. "*Kiss me*."

Dear Reader,

I'm delighted to lead off the MANHUNTING...
miniseries, because I've been there. I spent so
many dateless Valentine's Days that on one of
them, my father gave me a book—*How To Get a
Teenage Boy and What To Do With Him When You
Get Him* by Ellen Peck. I guess he was afraid I'd
never get married. That's why I can sympathize
with Hayley. However, since I was the one writing
Hayley's story, I made sure Hayley *found* a groom.
But you know what? I read the book my dad gave
me and the next Valentine's Day, I had a boyfriend.
Five years later, he was *my* groom!

Happy Valentine's Day, and good luck!

Heather MacAllister

Books by Heather MacAllister

HARLEQUIN TEMPTATION

543—JILT TRIP
583—BEDDED BLISS
010—CHRISTMAS MALE
637—BRIDE OVERBOARD
656—LONG SOUTHERN NIGHTS

Heather MacAllister

Manhunting
in Memphis

Harlequin Books

TORONTO • NEW YORK • LONDON
AMSTERDAM • PARIS • SYDNEY • HAMBURG
STOCKHOLM • ATHENS • TOKYO • MILAN
MADRID • WARSAW • BUDAPEST • AUCKLAND

For the world's greatest critique group:
Trisha Alexander, Amanda Stevens, Alaina Hawthorne
and Kay David

ISBN 0-373-25769-4

MANHUNTING IN MEMPHIS

Copyright © 1998 by Heather W. MacAllister.

This edition published by arrangement with Harlequin Books S.A.

® and TM are trademarks of the publisher. Trademarks indicated with
® are registered in the United States Patent and Trademark Office, the
Canadian Trade Marks Office and in other countries.

Printed in U.S.A.

_____Prologue_____

HAYLEY PARRISH STOPPED in front of a booth and gazed around the crowded Versailles Ballroom of the famous Peabody Hotel where bridal industry exhibitors vied for the attention of hundreds of future brides and their mothers. Banners reading Love Is In The Air At The Memphis Bridal Fair hung from gilded mirrors and over a raised platform in front of a projector screen.

"Hayley, doesn't the sight of these gorgeous wedding dresses make you want to nudge that man of yours into setting a date?"

She looked down into the hopeful eyes of her mother, Lola, who was fingering different weights of white satin swatches. "We're not ready to set a date yet, Mama."

"Once you hook a fish, it isn't good to wait too long before you reel him in," replied her mother. "You're twenty-five. Time is growing short if you want to wear white. In fact..." She held the swatches next to Hayley's face. "No, you're still all right as long as you remember to moisturize around your eyes. Once those little lines appear, you'll have to wear eggshell or candlelight."

Hayley wasn't about to get into a discussion of white and its appropriateness for her wedding dress. "I can't get married without a groom, Mama, and Sloane's job will keep him in El Bahar for several more months."

Her mother dropped the swatches with a genteel sound of disgust. "*How* many more months?"

"I don't know." Hayley led her mother away from the Betty's Bridal Barn booth. "Just remember that he's earning a nest egg for us."

Her mother arched an eyebrow. "Are you sure he hasn't flown the coop?"

"Mo-ther!"

"Well, can I meet him sometime at least? I swear, Hayley, if I didn't know better, I'd think you made him up."

Since that was precisely what Hayley had done, she distracted her mother by pulling her over to a booth that specialized in butter mints custom dyed to match the bridal colors.

It worked.

"Oh, look!" Her mother held up a black ruffled paper cup. "Isn't this just *precious?*" The white mints inside sported black bow ties.

"That was a favorite with brides who had black and white weddings, though that scheme isn't as popular now," the booth attendant explained.

She and Hayley's mother pored over a catalog devoted to butter mints, thus sparing Hayley the necessity of manufacturing more details about the mythical Sloane Devereaux.

She remembered the night over a year ago when Sloane was born. She'd just returned from a date with a man who had a relative who knew someone who lived next door to the niece of a woman who played bridge with her mother. Hayley's mother was desperate for her to meet a man and get married, and for the sake of their relationship, Hayley occasionally broke down and accepted a maternally arranged blind date. This was one of those breakdowns.

The man was named Morris. Hayley had decided not to hold that against him.

Morris was eighteen years older than she was. Hayley liked mature men.

Morris was shorter than she was. Hayley was tired of wearing high heels anyway.

Morris liked to dance. Hayley decided he had possibilities and wore her flats.

Unfortunately, it soon became apparent to Hayley that the reason Morris liked to dance was that dancing provided an opportunity for groping, no doubt the only opportunity Morris could get.

Once a slow number began, Morris planted both hands on her bottom and yanked a surprised Hayley toward him. His head rested just beneath her chin, conveniently against her breasts.

Nearly overcome with the smell from the dark "instant hair" he'd used to camouflage his bald spot, she'd endured one dreadful dance, trying to hold herself away as he'd nuzzled ever closer.

After escaping to the ladies' room, she'd been trying to think of a tactful way to bring their evening to a close, when she'd seen herself in the mirror.

Black smudges and speckled bits of "instant hair" adorned the bodice of her new white silk blouse and the skin at her throat where Morris had rubbed his head.

Hayley had abandoned Morris, returned home and promptly invented Sloane Devereaux, named after a character in a book she'd just read.

Sloane saved her from the Morrises of the world while giving her the unexpected bonus of an improved relationship with her mother. Now that Hayley, the youngest of the three Parrish girls, was supposedly engaged, she and her mother had never been closer.

Hayley loved her mother, and she knew her mother loved her, but they were two entirely different people—in both looks and temperament. Each accepted, but didn't quite comprehend, the other.

But the instant Hayley had intimated that she and Sloane had come to an "understanding," it was as though she and her mother had at last reached the common ground they'd sought. Any previous differences no longer mattered, and Hayley didn't want to jeopardize this new rapport with her mother. So if one of the consequences of faking a fiancé was blowing a Saturday at the annual Memphis Bridal Fair, then Hayley was willing to make that sacrifice.

She smiled fondly as her petite, Southern belle mother collected a business card from the butter-mint woman. Planning every detail of Hayley's wedding was Lola's new mission in life—one she'd obviously been looking forward to.

Hayley wasn't too concerned about all that planning going to waste. Eventually she'd break up with Sloane, citing the strain of the long separation on their relationship, but only after she found a substitute fiancé—a real one.

"Hayley, I've got extra entry forms for the wedding contest." Her mother stopped in front of a catering booth and took two samples of punch, handing Hayley one.

"I've already entered." Hayley accepted the punch, but waved away the entry forms for the Sweetheart Valentine Wedding, the grand prize of the Memphis Bridal Fair.

"But only once. When I was here with your sisters, we filled out at least a hundred forms."

That's because my sisters wanted to win, Hayley thought, shuddering at the memory of the elaborate stage shows that had been the other Parrish weddings.

Her mother sipped from the tiny paper cup. "Hmm. The mango makes the punch too pulpy but the color is perfect for bridesmaids' dresses," she noted. "And at your sisters' weddings, the bridesmaids' dresses matched the punch."

The implication was that it would be the same for Hayley.

Any comparison with her older sisters, Gloria and Laura Jane, who were married replicas of their mother, was a sore point with Hayley, who was a female version of her tall, brown-haired father.

She missed her father—missed the closeness and the way they understood each other. Though he'd died when she was still in school, Hayley didn't think he'd be worried that she'd reached her mid-twenties without marrying. However, her mother took it as a parental failure on her part that Hayley was still single.

Hayley wasn't against marriage. Far from it. She just hadn't found the right man. And frankly, there was no hurry. She liked being engaged. Friends and relatives had stopped flinging men her way, so Hayley didn't have to fling them back anymore.

But heaven help her if her mother ever found out what she'd done.

"Let's fill out a few more entry forms," Lola suggested. "They'll be closing the box soon."

Hayley sucked the mango pulp from between her teeth. "Isn't entering more than once cheating?"

"Hayley, this drawing is for the wedding of your *dreams*." Lola tossed their cups into a white trash receptacle adorned with a satin bow. "Remember, all is fair in love and war."

"I expected a lot more love and a lot less war," Hayley murmured, watching brides and their mothers crowd around the booths.

"Then you've never tried to book a popular caterer for a weekend in June."

No, she hadn't. And she wouldn't for this June, either, no matter how much her mother might want it.

"A girl's wedding is the single most defining moment of her life," Lola said. "Her husband's, too. You want a *serious* event, Hayley—so serious that your husband has no doubt that he now *is* a husband."

Serious weddings equaled serious expenses, Hayley thought. When the time for her wedding actually arrived, she was going to have to convince her mother to scale down. She was *not* going through the same circus her sisters had. They'd reveled in the attention. Though the details of their weddings had been discussed incessantly for months, Hayley still didn't understand why it was necessary to collect twenty-seven shades of blue from which to choose dresses, ribbons, napkins and matchbook covers.

"Write, Hayley." Her mother curled Hayley's fingers around a gold pencil with Hiram's Catering embossed on it, and positioned it over an entry form.

To please her mother, Hayley started writing.

At that moment, an announcement interrupted the sappy ballads that had been playing all afternoon. "Ladies, if you will make your way to the podium, we're ready to have the drawing for the winner of the Memphis Bridal Fair Sweetheart Valentine Wedding!"

"And you've only entered once, Hayley," Lola fretted.

"Mama, it's okay."

Hayley and her mother swam into a pastel tidal wave that lapped at the edge of the platform. A tuxedo-clad disc jockey launched into an innocuous patter as two models emptied the box of entry forms into a clear, plastic ball.

"Give it a good spin there, girls," he directed, then turned to a smiling couple at his side. "Let me introduce our guests of honor, Mr. and Mrs. James Martinez, winners of last year's Valentine's wedding."

The couple beamed at the swell of enthusiastic applause.

"So how's married life?" The DJ thrust a microphone at Mr. Martinez.

"Fine."

Mrs. Martinez elbowed him.

"Wonderful. It's wonderful. I'm *real* happy."

Mrs. Martinez smiled.

"You two were actually married last month on Valentine's Day, right?"

They nodded.

The DJ faced the matrimonial hopefuls. "As you know, there are lots of extra goodies in store if you can wait until Valentine's Day to get married."

Giggles rippled through the crowd.

"Now, our cameras captured some of those special moments leading up to the Martinezes' big day."

On cue, the lights dimmed and the slide show began.

"To celebrate their engagement, our couple dined at the exclusive Justine's restaurant..."

Oohs and aahs sounded as a slide of Mr. and Mrs. Martinez being served champagne flashed on the screen.

The next slide showed a stiffly posed Mr. Martinez slipping an engagement ring onto his fiancée's finger. "And to seal the engagement, you might use your thirty-percent-off coupon to select a ring from Robertson's Fine Jewelry."

"With the markup on diamonds, you'd think Robertsons's could have offered *fifty* percent off," Lola said, then patted Hayley's arm. "But that will be Sloane's problem." Her mother's gaze briefly dipped to Hayley's naked left hand.

Hayley had no intention of buying a fake ring. Her mother could spot a cubic zirconia at twenty paces.

"Gift certificates from Marnie's Gifts and Slocum's Jewels will come in handy when you choose mementos for the wedding party."

A slide showing gold cuff links and silver bangles was next.

Her mother sighed. "Couldn't you just die?"

Hayley did feel dazzled as slide after slide illustrated the couple selecting furniture and household appliances, china, silver and crystal, or modeling outfits from his-and-hers trousseaux. She'd forgotten that there were serious perks associated with getting married.

But even her sisters hadn't gotten the loot the Martinezes had.

"If you won, you'd be set for *life*," Lola whispered.

She wasn't the only one whispering, but everyone was awed into silence when the pictures of Mrs. Martinez's bridesmaids flashed onto the screen.

In keeping with the Valentine's Day theme, the bridesmaids wore long red velvet dresses and carried roses.

"Those nosegays alone must have cost a hundred and fifty dollars a piece," Hayley's mother murmured.

"There's enough velvet in those dresses to upholster a sofa," Hayley said.

The crowd gasped and broke into spontaneous applause when the slide of Mrs. Martinez in her wedding dress appeared.

"There isn't a square inch of her that isn't beaded or

crystaled," Hayley's mother unnecessarily pointed out. "She wasn't about to be upstaged. Remember that, Hayley." Approval sounded in Lola's voice.

"Don't you think the dress is…excessive?" The elaborate dress was for someone who enjoyed being the center of attention. Someone completely unlike Hayley. "Add some feathers on her headpiece and she'd look right at home in Las Vegas."

"Hush," Lola scolded. "You don't have to choose the exact same dress. The idea is to wear a dress equal to the scope of the wedding."

Hayley detected future clashes with her mother on this scope thing. "Okay, but I'm not wearing a dress that makes me look like a sequined marshmallow, and I don't want my bridesmaids looking like sofas in a Victorian bordello." She might as well make a stand now.

"Of course not, sweetie," her mother said placidly.

That was too easy. Hayley wondered just exactly what sort of bridal regalia her mother had in mind for her. Not that it mattered, since any wedding discussion was academic at this point.

Hayley found herself wishing that she and her mother were really planning her wedding. The crowd was full of nervous anticipation as mothers and daughters clutched each other and crossed their fingers, and Hayley would have liked to share the feeling with her mother, as her sisters had done.

Instead, her feet hurt and she wanted to go home.

Pictures of the reception flashed on the screen.

Lola smiled at her and crossed her fingers.

"...fabulous reception aboard the *Mississippi Princess* paddle-wheel steamer, where you and your guests will sail down the river to historic *Vicksburg, Mississippi!*"

Squealing. Clapping. Little hops up and down.

"From there, you and your groom will continue on to New Orleans, and then you're off on a honeymoon cruise to Puerto Rico!"

Screams. Wild applause.

"A *cruise!* Oh, Hayley, cruises are so romantic!" Her mother was clapping with the best of them. "It would be the perfect honeymoon for you and Sloane."

A cruise in February sounded mighty fine to Hayley. In fact a honeymoon anywhere they served drinks with little umbrellas would do. She was beginning to have a serious attack of self-pity.

"And now, may I have a drumroll, please?"

The drummers in three of the bands demonstrating their music obliged.

The models twirled the plastic ball one more time. The DJ opened the door.

Mrs. Martinez reached in past her shoulder and pulled out a slip of paper.

Nervous giggles sounded as the DJ milked the moment. One of the drummers dropped out.

"And the winner of the ultimate, the fantastic, the unbelievable Sweetheart Valentine Wedding of her dreams is...*Miss Hayley Parrish!*"

How odd, Hayley thought, there must be another Hayley Parrish at the bridal fair.

Her mother screamed in her ear and burst into tears. One of the bands began playing a disco version of the wedding march, while another played "We've Only Just Begun." Inexplicably, the third launched into "Raindrops Keep Falling on My Head."

"Hayley, c'moooon down!"

With stunned astonishment, Hayley realized she'd won. With her mother pushing, she made her way to the platform and up the steps to the sound of polite, though restrained applause. Her ears were still ringing and she had trouble hearing. Then she was nearly blinded by a spotlight.

"So, Hayley, congratulations! Is your fiancé here with you?" The DJ shoved the microphone in her face.

"No," Hayley answered, mesmerized by the sea of envious brides pouting before her.

"Have you set a wedding date yet?"

"No."

The DJ leaned close in pseudoconfidentiality. "Do you think you can talk him into having the wedding next Valentine's Day and collecting those extra goodies?"

Hayley smiled weakly. "Waiting won't be a problem."

No, she had a much bigger problem. Standing by the edge of the platform, Lola looked as though she'd seen the gates of paradise. Tears glistened on her cheeks.

And at that moment, Hayley knew she was going to devote the next eleven months of her life to finding a man to marry on Valentine's Day.

Two months before Valentine's Day

HAYLEY PARRISH WAS a woman with a wedding—a wedding and no groom.

And it was time to tell her mother.

Yes, after spending months eliminating all the bachelors at McLauren Industrial Services, where she worked as a technical writer, at three church singles' groups and on the Internet, Hayley was going to throw in the towel, or the ring or whatever it was a woman threw when it was apparent that fate had decreed that she remain single for the time being.

She'd tried—she'd really tried—to find someone, but since the time had come to place concrete orders for wedding goods, and Hayley didn't have a concrete groom, she was going to have to tell her mother that she'd broken up with Sloane and regretfully give back the wedding.

There was bound to be weeping and wailing and gnashing of teeth, but wasn't that why she'd left an icy pitcher of margaritas in her apartment refrigerator?

The sooner she delivered the news, the sooner she could slurp margaritas.

"Mama, Sloane and I had a fight."

Hayley and her mother had just finished their weekly Saturday lunch and were sitting at the dining room table in the house where Hayley had grown up.

"I thought you were acting a little preoccupied. Well, don't worry. All engaged couples have these squabbles, Hayley." Lola opened a bridal magazine to a page she'd marked. "It's due to the stress of planning the wedding."

"Sloane hasn't been under any stress," Hayley pointed out.

"Of course, he has." Lola took off her reading glasses to stare at her daughter. "He must feel very frustrated to be all the way on the other side of the world and miss out on the wedding excitement. You should be more understanding." Lola put her glasses back on.

Hayley found herself resenting a person who didn't exist. She prepared to kill him off anyway. "He can't make it back in time for the wedding. And, under the circumstances, I feel that—"

"Nonsense. It's his *wedding* after all. I'm sure if he properly explains the situation, he can schedule a vacation. He's been gone for over a year. He must have a lot of time saved up."

"Yes, but his job is at a critical juncture—"

"He's known about this wedding for months."

"That's my point. If Sloane can't make time for a wedding, then he certainly can't make time for a marriage." Hey, that sounded pretty good. "I think marrying him would be a mistake."

"He'll just need a little reeducation, Hayley." Lola paged through a different magazine, then turned it to show her daughter. "What do you think of these bridesmaids' dresses? I believe they're the same as the ones in that issue, but without the bows in the back. Now, I like a pretty bow in the back. It adds interest for the guests, and your sisters are slim enough to carry them off. If there is anything less flattering than a bow unable to lay flat, bouncing around as the bridesmaid does the hesitation step down the aisle, I don't know what it could be."

"Being jilted." Hayley propped her chin on her fist. Her mother wasn't listening. "He's not going to show up."

"Oh, Hayley." Exasperated fondness sounded in Lola's voice. "I don't think there has ever been a bride who didn't mentally touch on the possibility." She pointed to the lingerie catalog from the store where Hayley had won a two-hundred-and-fifty-dollar gift certificate. "We'll go shopping and spend your gift certificate. Then you make sure Sloane comes back a week ahead of the wedding. A little reminder of why he's getting married won't hurt."

"*Mother!*"

But Lola merely gave her an arch look that she never would have given Hayley before her "engagement."

The loss of this close relationship with her mother would be the worst fallout from doing away with Sloane. That, and giving up being the envy of her sisters for the first time in her life. But they'd been happy for her, too, and were expecting to come to Memphis for the wedding. Her mother had been looking forward to the family reunion. Nuts.

"I nearly forgot!" Lola jumped up, ran back into her bedroom and returned waving swatches of fabric. "Dusty rose velvet and ecru lace! Isn't it *perfect?*"

Hayley gazed into her mother's animated face and realized that she might have to spread the news of her "breakup" with Sloane over two visits. Today she'd lay the groundwork. But next week, for sure, Sloane would be history.

"Valentine weddings are always red and white or burgundy or wine—but pink velvet will acknowledge the day and look ahead to spring." Lola spread the lace over the velvet. "What do you think? Don't you just love it?"

"I think it's beautiful, Mama," Hayley said, just so she could watch her mother smile. The delicate colors would set off Lola's blond coloring. Her sisters', too, come to think of it. Hayley, a brunette through and through, needed more oomph.

But since the wedding wasn't going to happen, Hayley could be generous now.

"We have to decide on the dresses today. The spring catalogs are already out and we won't be able to order these after Christmas. If you don't want to get caught in chiffon, we'll have to contact the bridal shop this week. As it is, we're cutting it close."

Hayley knew that. She was surprised she'd been able to put her mother off this long. "Just let me talk with Sloane first. M-maybe he hates pink."

"No one could hate this color." Lola held the pink up to herself. "I know I can find a crepe to match for my mother-of-the-bride dress. Oh, Hayley." Dropping the fabric, Lola gripped Hayley's hand, tears glistening in her eyes. "I know how hard things were for us financially after your father died, but I want you to know that I still managed to put aside some of the insurance money for your wedding. Your sisters had gorgeous weddings, and I wanted my baby to have a wedding she'd always remember, too, but I knew I could never have afforded... Well, when you won your wedding, it was an answer to my prayers."

"Mama..." Hayley didn't think she could feel any worse.

Naturally she was wrong.

"Once you're settled with Sloane, I'm going to take that money and move to Sun City, Arizona, with your grandmother."

"*What?*" Hayley had known her grandmother was thinking of moving there, but her mother, too?

Lola released Hayley's hand. "It's a lovely retirement community. The Lowes and the Darnells moved there two years ago."

"I remember."

"And Marjorie Dickinson has been sending me pictures and begging me to come visit her. I—I miss Marjorie."

Hayley felt horrible, selfishly horrible.

"Anyway, as you know, I've been worried about Maw Maw living all alone. And this house has so many stairs, it wouldn't be practical for her to live here. But now I can sell this big old place, and Mother and I can move to Sun City all because you won your wedding." Lola beamed. "Isn't it wonderful?"

The chicken salad they'd eaten for lunch threatened to make a reappearance.

No wonder her mother had been so desperate to get Hayley married off. Lola wanted to see Hayley, the youngest of her daughters, settled before she made any major changes in her own life. She was preparing to relinquish the responsibility for Hayley's happiness and security to Sloane. An old-fashioned attitude, but there it was.

Hayley was going to have to convince her mother that she could take care of herself. "Mama, you should move to Sun City even if I don't get married. You know, that fight Sloane and I had was...was a real doozy. I just don't see us getting back together."

Her mother's face paled so rapidly, that Hayley automatically tried to cushion the blow. "Or if we do, it might not be in time to get married on Valentine's Day. And if that happens, then we'll just have a small, quiet family wedding."

"You'll have no such thing."

"Mama, I couldn't enjoy having a big wedding if I knew you'd spent your savings on it."

Lola's brown eyes grew wide. "But it's wedding money. I—I just couldn't bring myself to use it for anything else. And I won't leave you all alone."

"I'm not alone. I have friends." A thought occurred to her. "Anyway, Sloane would have to go back to El Bahar after the wedding and I wouldn't be able to go with him because foreign women aren't allowed to live there. I'd be alone then, so whether or not I'm married shouldn't matter if you want to move to Sun City with Maw Maw."

Lola gave her a secretive smile. "Hayley, honey, it's time we had a little mother-daughter talk."

"We had one of those talks."

Lola shut the bridal magazines. "We've never had one of *these* talks." Her fingers edged toward the lingerie catalog.

Oh, no.

"Sloane may think he's returning to El Bahar, but if you orchestrate your honeymoon properly, then he won't stay there long."

Ohnoohnoohno.

Lola flipped open the catalog and pointed to a long white peignoir. "The wedding night, and thereafter to be worn only on anniversaries."

"Why?" The expensive gown would eat a huge chunk of the gift certificate—not that Hayley was going to spend any of it.

"Because it represents you as a bride, not as a wife, and you want to complete the transition to wife as quickly as possible."

As Hayley pondered the transition process itself, and whether or not she wanted it to be all that quick, her mother paged past the black gowns.

"Some unfortunate brides make the mistake of wearing something like these on the next night." Lola shook her head. "Black should never be worn earlier than the second week of marriage. It's even better to wait until the one-month anniversary. Just when your husband thinks he knows everything about you..." She leaned forward and lowered her voice. *"Black."*

"Black?" Hayley repeated.

"Yes. Black is the color of seduction. By then, you'll have been lovers for a month—" Lola closed her eyes and held up her hand. "And I don't want to hear about anything to the contrary." She opened her eyes and flipped through the catalog. "A bride shouldn't wear black until after a whole rainbow of experience."

A rainbow popped into Hayley's mind with a groom at the end instead of a pot of gold. "So, should I wear red, orange, yellow, green, blue, indigo and violet?"

Her mother looked startled. "Red on the second night? Oh, I think not. Red is playfully passionate. Wear it just before you wear the black. Now as for orange and yellow..." Lola looked doubtful. "They're difficult colors to wear. Perhaps peach..."

"No, Mama, you said rainbow and I flashed back to freshman earth-science class. You know, red, orange..."

Her mother looked at her as though an alien had inhabited Hayley's body. It was an expression Hayley hadn't seen since she'd invented Sloane Devereaux.

"It was a joke. Never mind."

Lola blinked in the strained silence that always followed these misconnections, then returned to the catalog. "Here's a lovely pink gown. It's nice to echo the wedding colors on the second night."

She'd made a mistake to leave the margaritas for later, Hayley thought. The next time she tried to announce her broken "engagement," she was going to drink them ahead of time. Maybe even bring a pitcher with her.

"Now isn't this just the cutest thing?" Lola pointed to his-and-hers pajamas. "Would Sloane look good in something like this?"

"I don't know." Hayley didn't want to think about lingerie anymore.

"Try to be more helpful, Hayley." Lola sighed in exasperation. "It's bad enough that I've never met my future son-in-law, but I haven't even seen a picture of the man!"

"I showed you a picture." Hayley had found a group photo of workers in front of a drilling rig. They were identically attired in baggy, dirty overalls, hard hats and grimy faces that emphasized their white grins. She'd indicated that Sloane was the second man from the left on the back row.

Or was it the second man from the right?

"I can't believe that's the only picture you've got. Why, he could be anybody!"

As Lola continued to mark pages for the rainbow of love, a plan—a face-saving, albeit expensive plan—formed fully whole in Hayley's head.

Her mother had never met Sloane Devereaux. No one had met Sloane Devereaux. He could be anybody.

All Hayley had to do was find someone to pretend to be Sloane Devereaux for a long weekend. Her mother could still plan the wedding, then Sloane would return to El Bahar and their marriage would go downhill from there.

But by then, her mother and grandmother would be living in Sun City.

The drawback to this plan was that Hayley would have to borrow money to cover the tax bill she'd owe on the value of the prizes. Her mother was oblivious to the taxes Hayley would have to pay, but Hayley vowed to carry that information to her grave.

But the pluses—oh, were there pluses. No more blind dates, unless she felt like it. No more humiliating cross-examinations. She'd get a lot of appliances and pretty underwear, a cruise and a happy mother.

Sure there were a few details to work out, but by and large, this seemed like the best solution. Lola wanted to see Hayley get married, so she'd see Hayley get married.

She smiled at her mother. "Okay, Mama. Now let's go back to those black outfits."

JUSTIN BROOKS OPENED the hood of his faithful, though oil-guzzling car, and pulled out the dipstick. The old jalopy had to hold out a few more months before he could afford to replace it.

By then, if all went according to his master plan, and there was no reason why it shouldn't, he'd have a new, high-paying job as a corporate attorney, and could go car shopping.

And then life as he wanted to live it would begin. Justin Brooks, former debt-ridden high school math teacher, now debt-ridden IRS tax attorney, would become Justin Brooks, yuppie corporate attorney, with a yuppie bank account, and a yuppie haircut and yuppie friends and a yuppie social life with yuppie women.

He would revel in meaningless yuppieism. He'd flirt with frivolity, dance with decadence and preach the virtues of paying full retail.

Justin smiled to himself as he wiped the dipstick and threaded it back into the crankcase of an engine that had run a hundred-and-twenty-two thousand miles. It would be a novelty to own a car in which both the air conditioner *and* the radio worked. His new car would have a CD player and—

"Yo, Justin!"

At the sound of his friend's voice, Justin peered out from under the hood. "What's up?"

Ross jogged to the apartment complex parking lot. "I've got an audition."

"Hey, great." Ross getting called for an audition was still an occasion for celebration. If he actually landed an acting job that paid money, Justin would personally spring for a six-pack of imported beer.

"So...can I borrow your car? Mine's got a flat."

Ross's car was in even worse condition than Justin's. "Here." Justin tossed him the keys. "The jack's in the trunk."

"I don't need the jack."

"Then how are you going to put on the spare?"

"What spare?"

Justin swallowed his irritation. Ross took too many chances. There was a difference between living life on the edge and foolishly dangling over that precipice. "You need new tires."

"Yeah, I know." Ross leaned over the open hood. "If I get this gig, I'll buy new ones, I swear."

Pulling out the dipstick again, Justin grimaced. "Look at that. A quart and half low this time." He shook his head and replaced the dipstick.

"So buy a new car."

"I can't afford a new car."

"You could if you'd quit doubling up on your loan payments."

Justin shot him a look.

"Oh, man, lighten *up*."

"I'll lighten up when the time is right, and the time will be right after I've paid off the last of my college loans."

Ross spread his hands. "That'll take another five years at least."

"Not if I can help it."

"Justin, you don't have to—"

"Yes, I do," Justin interrupted him. They'd had this argument before. Ross's money, or rather, Ross's *father's* money, was the collateral for Justin's law school loan. Justin intended to free the collateral as quickly as he could.

"All right, then at least buy a different car," Ross said. "You can afford that. Oh, and get a real babe magnet this time."

"I don't need a babe magnet."

"But I do, and I'll be borrowing it."

Laughing, Justin punched open a quart of oil and propped the can in a funnel. "I'm headed over to the office, so you'll have to settle for a ride to your audition."

"You're going in to work? Man, it's Saturday! You're not getting overtime for this, are you?"

Justin shook his head.

"Then what's the point? Kick back and relax. You're going to forget how."

"I'm fighting the computer and need the quiet time to see if I can figure out what's wrong."

"Let one of the technogeeks handle it."

Justin tapped the last drops of oil from the funnel and replaced the crankcase lid. "First, I want to make sure I didn't transpose numbers anywhere. The computer techs love to make you look stupid in their reports."

"So, can we leave soon? I'm supposed to be there by nine."

Justin slammed the hood of his car shut. "Anytime."

HAYLEY SAT on a cracked-vinyl green couch in the office of Lawrence Taylor's acting and modeling studio. Mr. Taylor wore a scarf around his neck and drank tea with honey and lemon, along with something stronger, Hayley suspected. His accent and trilling basso profundo intimated a career in the English theatre—the kind spelled with the last two letters reversed.

Hayley was in awe of the posturing Mr. Taylor, but not in awe enough to agree to hire any of the actors who'd read for the part of Sloane Devereaux.

They'd all needed lines. Hayley didn't have lines.

She wanted someone who could take the background she'd created for Sloane and improvise.

And what was this motivation thing they all kept talking about? Sloane didn't need any motivation. All he had to do was show up and convince Hayley's mother, her sisters and the bridal fair people that he was for real.

Mr. Taylor plucked an eight-by-ten glossy from the stack, hesitated, then showed it to Hayley.

A mildly attractive man with a goatee smiled back at her. She wasn't much on goatees, but she shrugged.

"I'll ask him to come in." Mr. Taylor strode—he always strode—to the door and flung it open, then paused for dramatic effect. "Mr. St. John!"

The man who entered was shorter than Hayley would have preferred Sloane to be, but she liked the banked alertness in his eyes. And he'd shaved off his beard.

"Hi, I'm Ross St. John." He shook her hand, then glanced toward Mr. Taylor.

"Ross, Ms. Parrish is casting the part of a bridegroom."

As she'd done eight times before, Hayley explained what she wanted and who Sloane Devereaux was. Each time she repeated them, the details of her mythical fiancé's life seemed thinner and thinner.

Mr. Taylor was barely able to contain his sneer.

Ross St. John was the first actor who hadn't demanded a script. "What kind of man is Sloane?"

"An imaginary man."

"And what did you imagine him to be?" he asked patiently.

Hayley had never thought about it, but with Ross asking leading questions, she managed to create a character she thought would please her mother. "And he should act like he's capable of taking care of me," she added. "My mother won't be content otherwise."

Ross nodded. "Do I need to wear a suit?" He straightened and subtly changed his body language and expression. "I can do suits."

He was wearing a knit shirt and khaki slacks, but somehow, he exuded all the arrogant competence of a captain of the industry.

"How did you do that?" she asked.

He gave her a smile that was both sweetly sad and wise. "My father."

He didn't have to say anything else. Hayley understood all. His father didn't understand him any more than her mother understood her. She smiled at Mr. Taylor. "I'll take him."

JUSTIN STARED into his closet and realized he didn't have any clean shirts, which meant he didn't have clean socks or underwear, either. Not surprising since he'd spent every waking moment at the IRS office during the past week and a half tackling the horrendous mess left by software incompatibility glitches. It should have been a painless upgrade, but no. It should have been a department-wide upgrade, but no.

It shouldn't have corrupted the data, but yes.

And that corruption was delaying the start of Justin's master plan. He wanted to start sending out his résumés, but couldn't until he knew which of the returns he'd given to the tax examiners had been incorrectly flagged. When he left this job, he wanted everything to be running smoothly. He didn't want it to appear that he'd bailed out when things got rough.

So now he had to run a couple of loads of laundry. Justin needed a break, anyway. Rather than sorting through his clothes, he simply picked up his entire hamper and a roll of quarters and headed for the apartment laundry room.

At seven-thirty in the morning, he should have it all to himself, but Ross had already staked out the only machine that didn't have balance problems and he was stuffing it full.

"Hey! He lives." Ross grinned at him.

"Barely." Justin looked at the second-best machine, which bore an Out Of Order sign. He ignored the sign and lifted the lid.

"Feel like gambling today?" Ross asked.

"Give it up. I recognize your handwriting."

"Did it occur to you that the machine might actually be broken?"

Justin pointed to the clothes Ross hadn't been able to stuff into the first machine. "Nope."

"I'm going to have to invest in a more official-looking sign."

"I'd let you have the machine, but I've got to get into work."

"What *have* you been doing?" Ross added liquid detergent with a lavish hand and closed the lid. He patted his pockets.

"Computer foul-up." Justin tossed him the roll of quarters.

"Thanks. I'll pay you back."

Justin waved it off and borrowed Ross's detergent. When he struck it big, he was sending everything out to be cleaned.

"Since you haven't been around enough to notice that *I* haven't been around, I'll just tell you that I got the gig."

For an instant, Justin forgot his problems and sincerely congratulated his friend. "A commercial?"

"No. I'm a groom. A bridegroom."

"You're getting *married*?"

"No. Heaven forbid, though the bride is cute in a dangerously marriageable way." He carried his clothes to the other row of washing machines and selected one that restarted if you banged it on the side during the rinse cycle. Ross liked extra rinsing.

"So it's a play?"

"A private production with print ads, lots of exposure for *moi* and kind of a pageant thing at the end."

Justin smiled to himself. "By 'pageant thing,' do you mean a wedding?"

"Yeah. It's great, man. A huge break. Plus, I'll be spending the weekend in the lap of luxury at the Peabody."

"Well, congratulations. If anybody deserves success, you do." Justin meant every word.

"I figured if I hung in there long enough, something would happen. So, would you bang a couple of times

on this machine for me? I'll be back to load the dryer."
Ross acted like this job was no big deal, but Justin
could tell how important it was to him.

"I'm not going anywhere. I'll load for you," Justin
offered.

"Great. I gotta go pack. "I'm making my grand entrance at one."

After Ross left, Justin sat in the hard plastic chair and
stared at nothing until it was time to bang on Ross's
machine. He loaded the clothes, splitting his between
three dryers so they'd finish quicker. Then he sat and
stared at the tumbling clothes, finding the rhythm restful.

He'd never expected to have a friend like Ross—they
were two completely different types. When he mentioned it to Ross once, Ross said he liked to hang
around Justin because Justin reminded him of the kind
of life he'd have if he couldn't make it as an actor. And
then he pointed out that Justin needed him for comic
relief.

Justin needed relief, all right. He'd stay at his current
position until May, he decided. And then...then he'd
hit the job market for sure. He had stellar credentials
and expected to be wined and dined. And he was going to enjoy it, too. Every minute.

That was the plan. That had been the plan since he
was fourteen and finally old enough to augment the
meager salary his single mother was able to earn. That
had been the plan when he'd given up basketball in
high school because he'd had to work a part-time job
with full-time hours. That had been the plan when he'd

bypassed fraternities and social clubs in college so he could work. That had been the plan when he'd taught high school and studied for his law degree at night so he could make a dent in his enormous student loans.

And then Ross, good old Ross, had cosigned for him when his credit was maxed out.

He owed Ross, big-time, and was glad things were finally happening for him, too.

The first of his three dryers buzzed, jerking Justin out of a lovely fantasy involving corporations slinging money at him.

He was quickly folding and hanging clothes when he realized that Ross's machine had quit again.

The second dryer stopped a full five minutes before it should have. Rather than take the time to run around to the other side, Justin stretched across and jiggled Ross's machine. The liquid detergent hit the floor and the lid bounced across the concrete.

Great.

And then the third dryer stopped. Justin decided to fold the clothes now and clean up the mess later.

"Do I have perfect timing, or what?" Ross appeared in the doorway.

"Or what." Justin continued to hang up shirts before they wrinkled. "Your load still has another twenty minutes. But that second machine never finished. I banged it once."

"No prob." Ross loped toward the washer.

As he rounded the end of the aisle, Justin remembered the spilled detergent, but before he could call out a warning, Ross's arms flew up, and he disappeared with a metallic thud as he hit a machine, followed by a sound that reminded Justin of old pumpkins smashed after Halloween.

"Ross!" Cursing himself for forgetting about the spill, Justin raced around the corner to find Ross sprawled on his back.

He wasn't moving.

"Ross?" Justin could barely speak.

Blood mingled with the dark blue detergent on the concrete floor. "Oh, my God." He peeled off his T-shirt and packed it around Ross's head, afraid to move him in case his neck was broken or his back was injured.

Justin swallowed dryly. *A broken neck.* And it would be all his fault.

There was a pay phone in the laundry, and he dialed 911, watching as the red soaked his shirt.

Head wounds bled a lot, he told himself. But if any bleeding was to be done, it should be Justin and not Ross.

ROSS REGAINED consciousness while the paramedics were sliding the stretcher beneath him. "My gig."

Justin's heart sank. Ross's big break wasn't supposed to be his head. "Don't worry about it."

"Wait—for me...."

"You're going to be fine."

"The girl..." Ross winced. "You gotta tell her...."

"Don't worry about it," Justin reiterated. "I'll follow the ambulance to the hospital."

"Pea—" Ross broke off and groaned as they lifted the stretcher.

"He must have to empty his bladder," a paramedic commented.

"Peabody," Ross managed as they shut the door to the ambulance.

Justin stood, shirtless, in the parking lot and watched the ambulance drive away. He wished the weather was colder so he would suffer as he'd made Ross suffer.

He had to get dressed. He had to get to the hospital.

And then he was probably going to have to find the actress Ross was supposed to meet at the Peabody.

HE WAS LATE. Twenty agonizing minutes late.

Hayley paced around the elegant atrium of the Peabody Hotel and tried to pretend she wasn't watching the door.

Her mother sat in a floral tapestry chair at one of the tables surrounding the fountain and did a much more credible job of appearing to take "Sloane's" tardiness in stride.

Her sisters, Gloria and Laura Jane, perched on the marble rim of the tiled fountain and flirted with the famous ducks.

How could he be late? Ross hadn't been late to any of their previous meetings. For someone who seemed to have a casual personality, he was remarkably punctual. And this was supposed to be their wedding rehearsal.

Outside the Peabody, the driver of the limousine that was to take them all to the dock to board the *Mississippi Princess* had just been asked by a doorman to move.

Transfixed, Hayley watched the escalating argument.

"Hayley, honey," called her mother, with an assessing glance toward the fountain and her older daughters. "Come sit beside me." She patted the chair next to her.

"But, Mama—"

"Sit down." Though spoken in a soft Southern drawl, it was nevertheless a command.

Hayley sat.

"Hayley, it does not do to give the appearance that Mr. Devereaux's absence has any more significance than a delay in his journey, which was why I questioned the advisability of scheduling the rehearsal so soon after he was to arrive."

Hayley should have thought of that. Great. Her careful plans were already unraveling.

Lola sipped from a tall, frosted glass. "I declare, the poor man will barely have time to wash off the dust from his travels."

Her mother was beginning to sound like a character from *A Streetcar Named Desire*. This was never a good sign.

"I couldn't help but notice that you have been more nervous than excited about being reunited with him." Lola cast a meaningful look toward the elevators, where two women waited. "And if I've noticed, you can be certain that Mrs. Dobson and the other members of the Thursday Musical Club have noticed, as well. If you do not wish to be the subject of speculative gossip during their meeting, then I urge you to relax."

"Relax? He's nearly a half hour late! How am I supposed to relax?"

Lola languidly raised her hand to signal a waiter. "Perhaps by joining me in a gin and tonic."

Hayley squinted at the liquid in her mother's glass. "I thought that was mineral water."

"So, I hope, do Mrs. Dobson and the other members of the Thursday Musical Club."

She'd driven her mother to drink gin in the early afternoon. Hayley could barely contemplate what would happen if the actor didn't show up and her mother thought she'd been jilted.

And if he didn't show soon, her mother would probably call the airlines and find out that no Sloane Devereaux had been a passenger on any flight from El Bahar, which she would interpret as meaning he was still in El Bahar, which meant he was indeed jilting Hayley, which would mean Hayley's mother would feel it was her duty to stay in Memphis and comfort her devastated daughter, which meant more blind dates, which meant Hayley would be right back where she started, except several thousand dollars poorer.

Hayley groaned just as a gin and tonic appeared in her line of vision.

She and her mother picked up their glasses, clinked them together and drank in a rare moment of perfect harmony and understanding.

A CONCUSSION. Justin had given his best friend a concussion.

Ross, who'd had to be restrained when he learned he wouldn't be leaving the hospital that day, had struggled with the nurses until Justin had assured him that he would try to salvage the situation with the bride.

Unfortunately, all the information Justin had to go

on was that Ross was supposed to meet her at the Peabody.

It was going on two o'clock, so Justin figured he was already late. He didn't know this woman's name, or what she looked like, or where they were supposed to meet, but he figured he'd look for an angry bridal-type female, who was bound to get angrier.

Skirting the valet parking attendants, Justin parked his smoking car in a lot reserved for employees, and walked into the lobby.

The Peabody was a grand old hotel, and Justin immediately felt underdressed in his jeans, wrinkled shirt and jacket, though many others were dressed similarly. He ran a hand through his hair and searched the lobby, hoping Ross wasn't supposed to show up in a meeting room somewhere in the hotel.

Did anyone look like she was waiting for someone?

Tourists photographed the ducks in the fountain as two blond women in dressy outfits looked on. One of them checked her watch, then made a comment to the other. They both glanced to their left.

Justin followed their line of vision. A businessman-type read a newspaper, and nearby, two women sat at a table.

The women were wearing pastels, one was older than the other.... A bride and her mother? It had to be.

Or maybe not. But he'd thought this was a production of some sort. He didn't know anything about the acting business, but he'd expected more people to be milling around. Where were the cameras and the lights? Maybe they'd sent everybody home when Ross hadn't appeared.

There was that limo waiting outside, though. Weddings and limos kind of went together in Justin's mind. And women in dresses in pale colors.

Justin started weaving between the tables, then stopped.

For all his disjointed jabbering, Ross had been adamantly clear about contacting "the girl." He'd said nothing about directors or camera people or producers.

Following his hunch, Justin changed directions and headed for the concierge desk and had "the party meeting Ross St. John" paged.

Then he waited.

"WILL THE PARTY meeting Ross St. John please come to the concierge desk in the lobby?"

Hayley nearly choked on her gin and tonic.

What was he doing? This wasn't the plan. Swooping in and dazzling her mother and sisters was the plan. Though the actor she'd hired wasn't physically the dazzling type, he'd been adequately charming during their rehearsals, and Hayley thought he could pull it off.

She had a bad feeling about this, and it had nothing to do with drinking on an empty stomach.

Carefully, as though her actions weren't prompted by the announcement, Hayley set her drink down and looked at her watch. "Mama, I'm going to call the airport and find out if Sloane's flight has been delayed."

Lola waved her away—or she could have been signaling for another drink.

Hayley escaped, first to the phones, in case anyone was watching her, then quickly made her way to the concierge desk.

There was no one there, or rather, a man was standing there, but Hayley knew he wasn't the one who'd paged her.

This was a gorgeous man. Hayley could tell even though he tried to hide his gorgeousness beneath a rumpled outfit that looked like he'd climbed out of bed—probably not his own—and pulled on the first clothes he'd stumbled across on the floor.

He had striking black hair, carefully mussed to go with his rumpled outfit, and was exactly the type of man she'd wanted to hire, but wouldn't have because no one in her family would believe she could attract such a man.

She could; she knew she could. Well, maybe she could, she thought, the closer she got to him and the better he looked. Then he caught her gaze and she was hit with the full force of unexpected blue eyes. Okay, maybe she could attract him if a good hair day coincided with a time when she wasn't recovering from a Mexican food binge bloat.

It had taken her all of her adolescence—and a nasty encounter with a home highlighting kit—to emerge from the shadow of her mother and sisters' blondness, and start concentrating on men who liked brunettes.

She wondered which type he was.

JUSTIN WATCHED the lone woman approach. She was the one who'd been sitting with the older woman, and he felt a momentary satisfaction at guessing right. She was pretty, in a quiet way—a normal way that was a relief from the more exotic artsy theater types Ross was attracted to and occasionally tried to fix Justin up with. But Justin liked women who wore their earrings in their earlobes and nowhere else, rings on their fingers and bracelets around their wrists.

He wasn't too keen on frizzy hair, either. This woman's hair, a rich brown, swung when she walked. Nice.

Very nice.

Cute in a dangerously marriageable way. That was how, this morning, Ross had described the woman he was working with. Justin could see him describing this woman as cute because Ross had a skewed sense of beauty. To him, wholesome meant bland, conservative was boring, and it didn't take a psych major to understand that he was attracted to women who wouldn't fit in with his wholesome, conservative family.

This woman would never pierce anything that wasn't meant to be pierced.

"Are you waiting for Ross St. John?" he asked before she spoke to the concierge.

Her frozen expression told him the answer before she stuttered her response.

"Y-yes."

Justin swallowed. "There's been an accident."

The blood drained from her face, throwing the freckles sprinkled across her nose into stark relief. "What happened?"

"He'll be fine," Justin quickly reassured her. "Eventually. He fell and hit his head, and he's got a concussion. He's in the hospital right now and, uh, well, he can't..."

Growing horror paled her face even more.

Justin hurried on. "The thing of it is, he'd be here if he could. He takes his acting commitments very seriously and I know he was looking forward to this...job. I don't suppose there's any way you can postpone whatever it is you're doing, for a couple of days?" It would probably be longer, but Justin wanted to buy time.

Her toffee-colored eyes were huge. "He was supposed to be my fiancé," she whispered.

"I know. He told me he was playing a bridegroom."

"Everything's all..." She drew a shuddering breath. "I need a fiancé and I need one *now*."

This was worse than he'd thought. "I'm sorry, but there's no way Ross is leaving the hospital anytime soon."

"Then what about you?" She clutched his arm in a death grip.

"Me?" Justin was floored. "I'm not an actor!"

"I don't care at this point. You're male and you're conscious. And right now you're all I've got."

"You don't understand. I'm just a friend of Ross's. I don't have any acting experience, so I can't—"

"You don't have to *act*. You have to pretend to be Sloane Devereaux, my fiancé."

Justin had no room in his life for a fiancée, pretend or otherwise. Fiancées weren't part of the plan. The plan was to date for fun, not date for marriage.

He had no idea what *her* plan was, but it sounded like it would interfere with his.

She misinterpreted his silence as contemplation. He wasn't contemplating anything, except how to pry her fingers off his arm.

"My mother and sisters are over by the fountain. They're expecting to meet my fiancé and go to the wedding rehearsal. The limousine is waiting. *Please.*"

"You mean you're trying to fool your family into thinking you're getting married? That's Ross's big acting job?"

She sighed. "Yes."

Justin went into lawyer mode. "I want no part of fraud, and I will so advise Ross."

After a surprised laugh, she said, "It's nothing illegal, I swear."

"Then where's your real fiancé?"

She closed her eyes and said tightly, "I don't have one."

"You mean you and...what's-his-name broke up?"

"Sloane." She opened her eyes again and gave him a look he couldn't interpret. "Something like that."

"Why don't you just tell them?" Justin gestured toward the fountain.

"That's not an option, or I wouldn't have hired your friend." She swallowed. "Look, I know you don't know me and I don't know you, but I really need your help. Please."

"I—"

"It's only until Valentine's Day. I'll pay you."

Justin stared into a pair of desperate brown eyes. He'd seen desperation before, in Ross's eyes just an hour ago, as a matter of fact, though the unequally sized pupils disguised it a bit.

Justin had been desperate before and recognized that this woman believed she was about to lose everything important to her. He knew that feeling, and he wouldn't wish it on anybody.

Her predicament was his fault. He'd put that desperation in her eyes. Due to his carelessness, he'd not only ruined Ross's big chance, such as it was, but her plans, as well.

He had to do something to make it right. He knew he did. The last time he was desperate, Ross had come through for him.

Now it was his turn to help Ross, and covering for him seemed to be the only way Justin could. It had nothing to do with her eyes, or her hair—okay, or even her freckles. He owed Ross.

"I've never done anything like this before." He exhaled. "It'll never work."

Relief flooded her eyes. "We'll make it work." Breathing deeply, she released the grip on his arm. "I really appreciate this."

And she smiled.

It was a great smile, even if it was wobbly at the edges.

They gazed at each other for a timeless moment and Justin had the oddest sensation that his master plan, the plan that had remained as clear and as sharp in his mind as his own name, had gone slightly out of focus.

He blinked.

She blinked. "Now, I'm...uh, going back over to my mother, and you come in the front door and wave at me or something—"

Justin touched her arm. "Too late. Don't turn around, but I think your mother and sisters are headed this way."

"Three little blondes?"

"Yeah."

"Quick!" She flung her arms around his neck. "Kiss me."

And so help him, Justin did.

The day had been hellish. He was still shaky over Ross's accident, and right now, holding another human being felt wonderful. Comforting. Nice.

The cold anxiety he'd been carrying around with him eased as he leaned into the kiss, giving it more weight and scope than was wise.

She was soft and warm and her arms were wrapped around him as she held him close and kissed him back.

When was the last time he'd exchanged more than a handshake with anyone? He'd never been a hugger, and it had been many months since a woman had wandered across the barren wasteland of his social life. Even longer since one had lingered.

He'd been working so hard for so long without any break, and now a warm and willing woman was in his arms.

And so he kissed her. Really kissed her. Kissed her

for all the nice girls like her he hadn't asked out because he had neither the time nor the money.

Kissed her to ease the panic he'd seen in her eyes.

But mostly he kissed her because he wanted to, and didn't feel like holding back anymore.

He drew his hands around her waist, then lifted one under her hair to cradle her neck, gently telling her she didn't have to pull away on *his* account.

She had a great mouth, as someone with her smile would, and he parted her lips with his, tasting lemonade with an interesting kick.

Oh, yes.

She made a little sound in the back of her throat and he felt the vibrations against his tongue and then all over him.

He hummed an answer against her mouth, feeling an elemental pride that indulged a part of him he'd ignored for too long.

Spanning the hand at her waist, he dipped it to the small of her back and pulled her closer, enjoying the way she fit against him.

Enjoying everything at this point.

Everything except when she stiffened and wrenched her mouth from his.

She stared at him, looking dazed and stunned, which was pretty much the way he felt. "You take direction *real* well," she gasped in a husky voice. "I like that in a man."

Gradually, awareness of his surroundings returned, element by element. First color, then shapes, then shapes that moved, then shapes that spoke.

"Hayley, honey, I *assume* this is your Mr. Devereaux."

Hayley. Her name was Hayley. He'd better not forget, he thought, as he looked into the assessing eyes of Hayley's mother.

Hayley said nothing, and he got a kick out of knowing he was responsible. Then a reality check followed when he realized he had to pull this off for her and for Ross. He felt her quiver and slipped a supporting arm around her.

Charm was called for here. "Call me Sloane, ma'am." He put a little extra into his smile.

She dimpled and looked at him from under her lashes. "Sloane." The word rolled off her tongue. "And I'm Lola. Hayley, you'll want to introduce Sloane to your sisters."

Thus prompted, Hayley came to life and introduced him to the two pastels. The older blonde eyed him with more interest than Justin thought a sister should. Her eyebrow rose slightly.

Way more interest.

He dimmed the wattage on his smile and squeezed Hayley's waist. When she looked up at him, he dropped an impulsive kiss onto her temple. Her cheeks pinkened. Good. She needed the color.

He glanced back to the sister. *Get the message, Blondie?*

"Sloane, wherever is your luggage?" Hayley's mother asked.

Luggage? "It's...not here."

"The...airlines lost it," Hayley supplied.

"So *that's* why you were late," said Blondie.

Justin had already forgotten her name. He was going to have to start paying attention.

"We were beginning to wonder." Her expression and the expression of the other sister told him exactly what they were beginning to wonder. Justin winced inwardly for Hayley.

Lola tut-tutted. "Something like that was bound to happen. Are you up to the wedding rehearsal?"

"Sure," Justin said.

"NO," HAYLEY SAID. "Sloane should check into his room first so when they find his luggage, they'll have someplace to put it."

Her mind was finally beginning to work again after the shock of his kiss.

Those blue eyes...that black hair...that kiss.

Holy cow.

She felt like she'd already been through all the colors of the rainbow. She was ready for black.

Where had he been when she'd scoured Memphis for men?

What makes you think he's available?

Ohmigosh. What if he's married and he's wearing a wedding ring?

No. Hayley instantly relaxed. Not only would her mother and sisters have noticed—and commented—on a ring, but married men didn't kiss the way he'd just kissed her, or rather, they didn't kiss women that way who weren't their wives.

Frankly, there was bachelor hunger in that kiss.

Fate was demonstrating a quirky sense of humor regarding Hayley.

But this wasn't funny. No, taking away her perfectly fine actor and substituting this gorgeous, sympathetic man was meant to torture her—punishment for lying, no matter how good or noble the cause. It didn't matter that Hayley had rationalized that she'd won a wedding, not a marriage. Lying was wrong and Hayley knew she'd have to pay, but she thought her payment was going to be to the IRS.

Fate was toying with her before exacting payment. Just when Hayley thought all was lost, fate sent her a man who might have been made to order from her dreams. And then fate had him kiss her.

Okay, that had been Hayley's idea, and a darned good one, if she did say so herself.

"Hayley, since we're so far behind schedule, I believe if Sloane is ready to go to the rehearsal, then we really should go," her mother said.

Hayley knew they should. The *Mississippi Princess* was due to start boarding for their dinner cruise at five o'clock. But she needed to talk with...with... She stared at him, realizing that she didn't even know his real name. She'd just have to think of him as Sloane.

"I do need to make a phone call first." Smiling, he excused himself and headed for the pay phones.

The four women watched his jeans-clad rear as he walked away.

Four identical sighs wafted through the lobby of the Peabody Hotel.

"No *wonder* you waited for that man." Lola fanned herself. "He's well worth waiting for."

"And he's devoted to her," Gloria said. "I gave him one of my aren't-you-just-the-cutest-thing looks and he didn't even give me so much as a 'thank you, ma'am' back."

Hayley turned to her. "You flirted with my fiancé?"

"It was just my little test." Gloria waved her hand. "He passed." But she didn't sound pleased.

Hayley knew all about Gloria's little tests and she'd endured enough of them.

Gloria was never satisfied until she had proof that a man found her attractive. The fact that Sloane hadn't responded as Gloria wished meant she'd probably try again. Hayley didn't want her trying again. "Well, you go play school in somebody else's classroom!"

"Hayley!" her mother interjected. "Gloria was only being friendly. She *is* the matron of honor, after all."

Hayley hadn't ever asked Gloria to be the matron of honor. As the oldest, Gloria had appointed herself, and Hayley hadn't felt like making an issue over it. Now she met Gloria's eyes. "I'm not blond, busty and beautiful, but I make up for it by being brunette and belligerent." She jerked a thumb over her shoulder. "So back off. He's mine."

The fact that Laura Jane, who had still been discreetly drooling in Sloane's direction, now no longer faced the telephones, Lola's eyes had widened and Gloria's lips were quivering told Hayley that her faux Sloane was probably right behind her and had heard everything she'd said.

Her suspicions were confirmed when his hands dropped onto her shoulders. "I like the sound of that."

Hayley liked the sound of it, too. She absorbed the warmth and weight of his hands, and the solid feel of him standing right behind her. He was on her side. She needed someone on her side.

And, too, seeing the envious looks on her sisters' faces went a long way toward healing the wounds she'd acquired in the dating wars during the past year. The actor she'd hired had been good-looking, but didn't have the same physical presence his friend did.

But this man was only playing a part, and forgetting that could inflict the deepest wound of all.

"Shall we get going?" Lola asked.

Hayley went on full alert. Treacherous waters ahead, and she wasn't thinking of the Mississippi.

They walked across the lobby, Hayley on one side of Sloane, Lola on the other.

"Sloane, I hate to bring this problem up when you've just arrived, but did you ever receive the invitations Hayley sent you?"

And so it began. "Mama, I told you that it takes several weeks for mail to reach him, and that Sloane was working out in the field."

Her mother looked horrified. "Do you mean to say that he didn't send out any invitations to the wedding?"

"Not many," he said.

Hayley poked him with her elbow.

"Hardly any at all," he added.

"This is awful. We haven't heard from *anyone* on Sloane's side of the family!"

"My family isn't close," he said.

Why wouldn't he just keep his talented mouth shut? "Now, Mama, I told you that Valentine's Day was going to be difficult for Sloane's schedule. We should be grateful he managed to make it at all."

"But...but this is his *wedding*."

"My parents are very sorry they can't be here," he said. "They're—"

"They're dead," Hayley interrupted.

"So naturally we didn't expect them," Lola said.

"I was going to say that they'll be here in spirit," he continued.

"And since he doesn't have any brothers or sisters, they won't be here, either." Hayley concentrated on feeding her fake Sloane information and didn't pay attention to how it sounded.

"In just a few days, Sloanie will have two brand-new sisters and brothers-in-law," Gloria chirped from behind them.

"And he won't be all alone in the world anymore," Laura Jane added, her voice just as lethally sugared as her sister's.

"He'll have a wife, too." Hayley was afraid the stiffness in her jaw sounded in her voice. *Sloanie.* Ick.

"Yes, but what about your friends? Isn't there *anyone* who is coming to the wedding?" Lola asked.

"My friends are all back in...the field...." Sloane cast Hayley a questioning look.

Oops. She'd been thinking about her sisters. "Yes, they're still in El Bahar."

"And send their regrets," he added.

"We'll have to instruct the ushers to seat some people on your side," Lola said serenely, and Hayley exhaled.

They'd reached the limousine. The driver opened the door. Hayley hustled Sloane around to the other side. "Just say as little as possible until I get a chance to brief you!"

He looked exasperated. "You could jump in a little quicker with clues!"

The driver opened their door and both pasted on quick smiles.

After seeing how everyone was seated within the car, Hayley climbed in beside her mother and Sloane sat beside her, directly across from Gloria.

Gloria crossed her legs.

Hayley narrowed her eyes.

"Well, Sloane," Gloria said, drawling his name into about fifteen syllables, "tell us every little thing about El Bahar."

"Well…" He chuckled. "Where to start?"

Hayley mentally castigated herself for not anticipating the question and tried to remember everything she'd read about El Bahar, which wasn't much. "You went on and on about the heat."

"It's very hot," he agreed.

"And the desert."

"It's sandy," he said. "Lots of sand. Miles of it."

"And, of course, you talked about the oil fields."

"It's a very oily country."

Hayley didn't need to see the blank stares and cautious nods to know that this wasn't working.

"What exactly did you do over there?" Hayley's mother asked.

"Cost analysis," he answered.

"He's an engineer," Hayley said at the same time.

Sloane looked down at her and she realized that he'd been thinking ahead and was trying to find a subject he could discuss on his own.

"I'm a cost analysis engineer." His look dared Hayley to disagree.

"And a very good one." Hayley patted his knee. When she saw Gloria's gaze drop to her hand, Hayley left it there.

"Well, I have no doubt of *that*." Lola cleared her throat. "So you work with numbers. That sounds like a job you could do anywhere—say, right here in Memphis."

"Ye-"

Hayley squeezed his knee.

"Yes, cost engineers are based everywhere. In my case, I'm based in...ah..."

"El Bahar," Hayley said distinctly.

"But you're so clever, Sloane. I just know you could think of a way to do your work here. After all, you're going to be a married man soon."

Sloane didn't respond, other than to smile, for which Hayley was grateful.

She didn't know how her mother was taking all this, but her sisters had exchanged discreet whispers, and

Gloria studied Sloane like a cat watching a bird with a broken wing.

During the rest of the ride, Hayley intercepted or deflected questions on Sloane's background, how they'd met and his plans for the future.

"Hayley, sweetie," her mother whispered in her ear at one point, "you need to calm down and let your man have his time in the sun. Men like to talk about themselves."

"So what did you think when Hayley told you she'd won a wedding?" Gloria asked.

"I was very surprised," Sloane said.

"We all thought it was a good thing, since you two had been engaged for so long," Laura Jane offered with a sly smile.

"Hush, girls," Lola admonished.

To her mortification, Hayley felt her face heat. She felt firm but gentle fingers tilt her chin until she faced him.

"A long engagement? Whatever was I thinking?" he murmured.

His tone was an audible caress, his gaze a visual one, and it was all for her sisters' and mother's benefit.

Real honest-to-goodness tears stung Hayley's eyes. What a sweetheart. He didn't know Sloane wasn't real. He thought he was helping a jilted bride avoid being embarrassed. There was no reason for him to help her, either. It wasn't his fault that the actor she'd hired hadn't shown up. He'd only come to tell her, and then she'd grabbed on to him and hadn't let go.

The car approached the docks and everyone looked

out the windows at the *Mississippi Princess* paddle-wheel steamer.

While the others were distracted, Hayley thought about what she'd done. She'd latched on to this man in desperation, and he'd dropped his plans for the day to rescue her. The only connection they had was the actor Hayley had hired. This man was honoring his friend's commitment, lucky for Hayley. He was truly one of the good guys.

They were little more than strangers, except for the eerie sensation Hayley got when she listened to him pretend to be Sloane. The way he took the information she fed him and embellished it—and she hoped he remembered all these embellishments—gave her a sense of getting to know the man, himself, rather than bringing Sloane to life.

At that moment, he looked down at her and gave her a reassuring wink.

She liked this fake fiancé of hers.

A lot.

3

Justin switched on the light in his apartment and headed toward his bedroom to pack.

This had been an interesting day. In an attempt to do laundry, he'd knocked out Ross and had become embroiled in a wedding scam. It was as though life had broken the hold Justin had put on it and had finally exploded in his face.

And he didn't care. To his surprise, he was having fun. He hadn't had fun for so long, it had taken him a while to figure out that's what he was doing. He knew that according to the master plan, it wasn't time for him to have fun yet, but he *enjoyed* pretending to be Sloane and fooling everybody. With each question came the danger of discovery and the rush afterward when he and Hayley escaped one more time.

Justin was good at acting, if he did say so himself. It was the attention to detail that was important, something Hayley didn't seem to grasp. For instance, why hadn't she hired anyone to be Sloane's wedding guests? Ross would know a dozen actors who'd do it for the free meal alone. Hayley hadn't even hired a best man.

Hayley. He liked her. Okay, he was attracted to her and she wasn't the type he wanted to be attracted to right now. He didn't even want to be attracted to her type when he could afford to. Her type was the marrying type. His type wasn't.

One day he would be, but marriage was an enormous responsibility that he wasn't about to take on yet. He'd end up resenting any woman who tied him down before he'd had a chance to fly.

He had no idea why Hayley was pretending to get married. Yes, he'd seen how her mother and sisters had weddings on the brain, but Hayley didn't seem to be the sort of woman to be cowed by them, unless she wanted to be. Must be an interesting story. He could hardly wait to hear it.

Justin couldn't remember the last time he had looked forward to a day. He'd called in and told his supervisor he was taking a long weekend off. The woman had sounded relieved. Maybe there was such a thing as too much overtime. Maybe they needed a break from him as much as he needed a break from them.

He stuffed a couple of clean shirts into a duffel bag, then stopped. Somebody flying into his wedding from overseas would have more substantial luggage.

Justin unpacked the duffel and dragged out his suitcases. He put a pillow into one and his clothes into another, then he changed the identification tags. He wasn't certain how she'd spelled Sloane, so he smeared the end a bit.

Details. It was all in the details.

Satisfied, he flipped off the light and headed to the hospital to see Ross.

IT WAS ELEVEN O'CLOCK at night and Hayley had a monster stress headache. She'd flung off her jacket, but otherwise had sprawled, fully clothed, on the bed in her suite at the Peabody. In her hand she clutched the business card of one Justin Brooks, IRS attorney.

At least she finally knew his name. And his occupation.

She groaned. She couldn't believe that she'd strongarmed an attorney to help her—or that he had.

They'd convincingly endured the wedding rehearsal and then dinner with her family, but he'd left to pack. She was now waiting for him to come back to the hotel so she could fill him in.

So far, she'd managed to explain away his vague and contradictory answers as jet lag, but truthfully, he was so good-looking and charming, her mother and sisters hadn't cared.

Hayley liked his approachable good looks. His generous nose saved his face from prettiness and his haircut said "barber" and not chichi stylist.

And, of course there was his incredible talent for kissing that she wouldn't think about because there wasn't much likelihood of it being repeated, more's the pity.

Hayley brought the business card to her mouth and rubbed the engraving across her lips, getting a little thrill when they tingled. Pathetic. Absolutely pathetic.

The door of the room next to hers opened. Hayley sat up. "Justin?"

"Or Sloane. Take your pick."

"Where have you been?" Hayley walked through the connecting door.

"Did you think I'd deserted you?" Justin carried his suitcases over to the luggage rack.

She sat on the bed. "No." Interesting. Justin not returning to the Peabody had not occurred to her. "You're not the type of person who'd run out on somebody."

"You're right, I'm not." Justin half smiled, half grimaced as he unzipped his suitcase. "But how do you know?"

"What do you mean, how do I know? I just do."

"I really want to know how you can tell. I'm getting ready to change my character type and I want to know the giveaways."

"Why do you want to change your character?" she asked, instead of answering his question. It was a stupid question anyway.

"I've been boringly steady and responsible for most of my life and I want to 'walk on the wild side' before I settle into responsibility for good." He hung up two pairs of pants, two shirts and tossed his socks and underwear in the drawer. "I want to be the kind of man who attracts a wilder sort of person."

"You mean women, don't you?" Hayley had a hard time keeping the sneer out of her voice.

"Yes. Shallow women who're interested in fun and aren't ready to settle down."

Well, that let Hayley out.

He gave her a sideways look. "I shouldn't admit that, should I?"

At least she knew exactly the type of woman he wanted. How disappointing. "A boringly responsible man wouldn't have."

He grinned. "Then there's hope for me."

Too bad there wasn't hope for her.

Justin held up a suit. "I didn't know if I'd need this or not."

Hayley waved it away. "You'll be fitted for a tux tomorrow. Oh, and I can either pay you in cash, or give you gift certificates to men's clothing stores."

It was Justin's turn to wave her offer away. "I'm not taking your money."

"But that's what we agreed."

Shaking his head, Justin stowed his suitcases. "You offered, but I agreed to do this because you were in a jam and Ross is in the hospital. He wouldn't calm down until I told him I'd talk with you. I just saw him, by the way. Had to sneak past the nurses."

Hayley imagined that all Justin would have had to do was throw a couple of smiles their way and he wouldn't have needed to sneak at all. "How is he doing?"

"He drifts in and out, but I think he understood the gist of what I told him." Justin had wandered over to the credenza and read the tag on the enormous fruit and snack basket. "'Congratulations and Best Wishes from the Management.' You're really going all out with this wedding, aren't you?" He studied the basket, trying to see through the plastic wrap.

"You're allowed to eat it, if you want," Hayley said.

"But if you don't want the chocolate, toss it my way. I already ate mine."

Justin dug in his pocket and removed a small pen-knife. "I see macadamia nuts. Trade?"

"Deal."

With the precision of a surgeon, Justin extracted the chocolate bar and tossed it to Hayley. She missed and it bounced on the bedspread.

The bedspread. She'd just walked into a virtual stranger's room and lounged on his bed. How very... relaxed of her.

Self-consciously she reached for the chocolate and stood, taking the opportunity to retrieve the macadamia nuts from her own basket.

When she returned to the room, she sat in a chair in the sitting area.

If Justin realized why she was doing so, he didn't let on. He'd been raiding the minibar and held up a bottle of fruit-flavored water. When she nodded, he carried over two bottles, then sat in the chair next to hers.

"Okay, talk," he said, getting to the point. "I've got to know why we're doing this." He opened the can of nuts and offered it to her, then leaned back when she declined.

So Hayley talked. She told him the story of winning the wedding and what it meant to her mother, going back and filling in the details while all he did was nod and crunch and not interrupt her. She felt such relief in telling someone, especially someone who listened without judging her. Ross had only been interested in the character of Sloane and not in the reasons for his creation.

"So what about this Sloane guy? Where is he?"

Hayley toyed with the idea of not telling Justin. Instead, she chose to avoid looking at him. "I made him up. He never existed."

The crunching stopped. "Did you make him up before or after you won the wedding?"

Hayley gave in, opened the imported chocolate bar and fortified herself with a mouthful of raspberry truffle. "Before. Long before."

"Why?"

"Because." How could a good-looking, apparently successful man like Justin understand? "Because I was tired of going on blind dates set up by my mother and her friends. Because I was tired of being questioned about why I didn't have a boyfriend and then being compared to my sisters and...then hearing my mother explain that I look like my father, as though it's a flaw I'll have to overcome." Hayley hadn't meant to say the last part. She hadn't even realized it herself until she'd said it.

She would have given anything—even the rest of the chocolate-raspberry truffle bar—to recall the words.

Now he'd feel obligated to make some remark about how pretty she was, and she didn't want a pity compliment.

She didn't get one.

"So you made up a guy to get your mother off your back." He resumed crunching. "Logical. I did the same thing once. Ross is always trying to fix me up. There was this actress friend of his." Justin stared into the can of nuts. "She never wore shoes." He looked up at Hayley. "I mean, never. Don't know how she got away with it onstage. I told him I was seeing someone at work."

"*You* had to make up someone? I can't believe you—I mean *any* woman would be thrilled to go out with you," she gushed, unprompted.

He smiled as he dug out the last of the nuts. "Thanks."

Wait a minute. Wait-a-minute. She'd just given him a version of the pity compliment she'd expected to receive.

And where was it? Rejecting a pity compliment wasn't satisfying if you never got it.

"So you made up this Sloane guy. By the way... *Sloane Devereaux?*" He shook his head. "Next time pick a regular name, okay?"

"There isn't going to be a next time," Hayley said distinctly.

"I guess not if you convince your mother you're married." Justin tossed the empty can into the trash. "Have you thought this all the way through? Now, a weekend is one thing, but I have to tell you, I'm not going to be able to bail you out during the holidays. Well, maybe Thanksgiving if you let me bring my mom and stepdad. We can tell everyone they're long-lost second cousins, or something."

"Your services won't be required on Thanksgiving." This conversation wasn't going the way she'd expected. "And for your information, I *have* thought things through. Sloane will be returning to El Bahar after the wedding."

"Without you?" He reached for his water and tilted the bottle to his lips. "Now *that's* unbelievable."

Amazing how a little offhand remark could bolster a woman's feminine self-confidence when a pity compliment wouldn't. Wondering if he realized what he'd said, Hayley glanced at him. His gaze flicked over her, then locked on to hers.

He knew.

They stared at each other in one of those silences in which a lot was said without anyone uttering a sound. Hayley was thinking about the rainbow of love and how it might apply to Justin.

Judging by the way Justin continued to watch her as he drank his water, he was thinking the male equivalent.

Where had all the air in the room gone?

"Well, Sloane's job... Women aren't allowed to live in El Bahar."

"What do they do with their women?"

She laughed too loudly. "I meant foreign women." Since when did she get rattled when a handsome man gave her the once-over?

"And how long were you planning to remain in this long-distance marriage?"

"Until my mother and my grandmother are settled in Sun City, Arizona. Mama won't leave until I'm married, and I won this wedding, so I'm going to use it."

"That's a lot of pressure to put on a daughter."

"Oh, no. She never would have told me. In fact, I

was ready to give the wedding back. It was just chance that she mentioned her plans before I did."

"Mmm." Justin set the bottle on the glass table. "You do know that you have to declare the value of your prize as income and pay taxes on it?"

Right. He worked for the IRS. "An agent explained it all at the time I won. But Mama doesn't realize this, and you're not to tell her. Otherwise, she won't use the money she's saved to move."

He twirled the empty bottle. "It seems like such a waste. It's too bad you aren't really engaged."

"Yeah." *And it's too bad we didn't meet months ago.*

If ever there was a chocolate moment, this was it. Hayley peeled back the foil and indulged.

"Couldn't you—"

"No." She swallowed. "No, I couldn't find anybody. And let me tell you, dating in this town when your mother is planning your wedding and all her friends know it, isn't all that easy."

A corner of his mouth tilted upward. "I can see that it wouldn't be."

"You have *no* idea," Hayley said, and bit off another hunk of chocolate.

JUSTIN IDLY TWIRLED the bottle, watching the cherries on the side rotate like they were in a slot machine.

Were the men of Memphis blind?

While he himself wasn't in a position to support a wife, Hayley was an appealing, wholesome, girl-next-door type with a quick and pretty smile, and a great mouth.

He remembered how that great mouth had felt against his and mentally deleted "wholesome" from the description, not that being wholesome was a bad thing, if it meant kissing the way she did.

Justin hoped that the women he intended to pursue could kiss like that. He certainly meant to find out.

He waited for the anticipatory zing he usually felt at the thought, and when he didn't feel it, he knew the blame lay at the feet of the chocolate-eating, bridal impostor sitting five feet away.

She and her kisses had stolen his zing. She'd spoiled him for the party girls of Memphis. No matter who he kissed from now on, he'd compare their kisses with hers. He should kiss her again. That first kiss must have been a fluke. He hadn't kissed anybody for a long time, and it was probably the act of kissing, itself, that had prompted his reaction, and not her in particular. A second kiss would verify his theory.

He half listened as she blathered on about photographs and luncheons and fittings, which he presumed were on the agenda for tomorrow.

He should lean across the space between the chairs and kiss her right now. Ross was always telling him he needed more spontaneity in his life.

On the other hand, she might spontaneously scream or slug him.

Maybe there would be kissing opportunities tomorrow. He could create some. If nothing else, there was always the "you may now kiss the bride" portion of the wedding ceremony. He'd kiss her then for sure.

The zing he felt at *that* thought zinged him right to his feet.

"What's the matter?" she asked, eyes wide, extremely kissable lips parted.

"I—nothing." It was the freckles. They fooled a man into thinking "wholesome" at first. Justin wasn't thinking wholesome now.

"Are you sure?"

Justin scrambled for something acceptable to say. "What about the ceremony? Is the judge clued in?"

"No. There isn't going to be a ceremony."

No ceremony? No kissing the bride?

"Right before, we'll have a fight and you'll go stomping off. I'll lock myself here in the Peabody and insist that Mama go on to the boat and see that everyone enjoys the cruise. I understand there'll be a fabulous buffet. Lobster, I think. Anyway, I'll leave a message at the hotel in Vicksburg telling Mama that we made up and eloped."

Justin had never before noticed how sensuous a mouth looked when saying the word *eloped*.

"I'll also mention that the fight was because you had to skip the honeymoon and go right back to El Bahar and I was trying to talk you out of it. You'll be gone when she gets back."

"And you won't get to enjoy any of the wedding?"

"I'm not doing this to enjoy the wedding. I'm doing this so Mama will believe the last of her little chicks has left the nest."

The plan was preposterous. She'd have better luck showing up at a tax audit without records. "Do you actually think your mother will leave you here and party down the Mississippi at what was to be her daughter's wedding reception?"

"She has a duty to her guests."

"But she'll be upset. You'll be upset. Everybody will be upset." And he—or Sloane—would come off looking like a first-class jerk.

Hayley sighed. "She'll do it to squash gossip."

Justin was all for that. Actually, not being seen by the wedding guests would be better for him. "But won't she be disappointed to miss her daughter's wedding?"

"She has plenty of experience at being disappointed in me."

There was a world of hurt behind Hayley's stark statement, more hurt than Justin could soothe with a few pat phrases.

He understood better than she'd guess. Right now she wore the same expression Ross did when he talked about his family. Justin wondered if Ross had picked up on the similarities. Probably, and that's why he'd been so determined to leave the hospital.

Justin sat on the arm of Hayley's chair. "I don't like Sloane very much."

"He apparently is the best I can do."

"If I thought you believed that, I'd be tempted to prove you wrong."

"And I'd be tempted to let you." She looked up at him.

He looked down at her.

It was the perfect cue for a kiss.

And the perfectly wrong time for it.

Justin wasn't available on any emotional level that mattered to her at this moment. At this moment, she was thinking marriage and all he was thinking of was a kiss.

So he stood and walked to the minibar, pretending to examine the contents. "You know, for a breakup fight to be believable, we'll have to show ahead of time that there's trouble in paradise."

She nodded. "Maybe you can keep excusing yourself to call El Bahar, or report that they've been calling you. I already stressed to Mama how difficult it was for you—Sloane—to get away. After all, none of your friends could."

He closed the minibar. "I meant to ask you about that. Shouldn't you hire some wedding guests for Sloane? It's going to look real strange that this guy can't drum up a single guest."

Hayley leaned her head back. "I couldn't afford to pay anyone. I've had to apply for loans to cover the taxes as it is."

At the word *loan*, Justin stifled the automatic clenching of his stomach. He hated being in debt. And at least he had his education to show for it. She'd have nothing.

"It's getting late and tomorrow will be crazy." She stood and stretched.

"Today had its moments." Justin tried to ignore the way her blouse stretched tight enough to outline the lace on her bra.

"Yes, but tomorrow the bridal fair people will be

running us all over town, taking our pictures for this year's brochure."

"What brochure?"

She dropped her arms. "For the Memphis Bridal Fair. Each year, the couple who won the wedding appears in the advertisements from the exhibitors who donated the prizes."

Lots of exposure for moi. Now Justin understood the appeal to Ross. But Justin didn't want exposure. "I can't be in the brochure."

"Why not?"

"I didn't win the wedding. You did."

"But you're the groom."

Justin tapped his chest. "I'm *not* the groom. I'm only pretending to be the groom."

"People won't know that."

"That's my point. Sloane may be going back to El Bahar, but I'm not. I live here. I work here. And I hope to date here."

"Oh." Her teeth tugged at her lower lip.

"Yes, 'oh.'" Did she have to draw attention to her mouth that way? He paced. "Hundreds of single women will see pictures of me as a married man." He stopped and pointed at her. "And you think *you* had trouble finding dates."

Hayley looked hurt. "Ross didn't mind about being in the brochure."

"Ross is a professional actor and model. Women know that."

"Well, tell the hundreds of single women you apparently want to pursue that we broke up."

"That'll make me look real good."

She smiled—no, that was a smirk. "You'll be using a different name. They won't remember."

"Yes they will. Women will think I changed my name so I can cheat on my wife."

"So you want to use your real name in the brochure?" Hayley walked toward the connecting door.

"No!"

"Then ask them to photograph you from the back. It's probably your best side anyway." She grinned over her shoulder.

"Oh, sure. Laugh it up. Your dating life isn't being ruined."

"What's left to ruin?" Sighing, she turned in the doorway.

Justin stopped short. "Hey. You'll find somebody."

She crossed her arms and leaned against the doorjamb. "That's what I keep telling myself, but I'm getting harder to convince."

As her gaze met his, there was another of those potent silences.

Tell her good-night and shut the door. "Good night," he said, but didn't shut the door.

She looked down at her foot, which traced the floral pattern in the carpet. "I'm sorry about you being in the brochure."

"Don't worry about it. I was teasing you. Those women are supposed to be engaged anyway," he said, before realizing it wasn't the best comment to make.

Hayley didn't seem bothered. "Thanks for doing this for me. I don't know what I would have done if you hadn't," she murmured, her voice so low, Justin had to take two steps forward and bend his head to hear her. "Ross has a very good friend." She raised her head unexpectedly, bringing her lips inches from his. "And I like to think I do, too."

The instant when he should have lifted his head came and went.

The instant when she should have pulled away came and went.

The only instant left was...

"Damn," he whispered, and kissed her.

Only their lips touched. He tasted the sweetness of chocolate and felt the warmth of her incredible mouth.

He could pull away now and call it a friendly goodnight kiss.

The instant when friendly became something more came and went and Justin was still kissing her. In fact, he now held her lightly by the shoulders.

Her arms uncoiled and she wrapped them around his waist.

How could he stop himself from drawing her closer?

Once more, he marveled at how right she felt in his arms. He could kiss a hundred women and not find one who fit as though she were made for him, the way Hayley did.

She tilted her head back and he felt the ends of her hair brush his hand.

He liked her hair and the way it swung when she moved her head, the strands flowing like heavy silk. Burying his fingers in it, he deepened the kiss.

The first kiss hadn't been a fluke and the second kiss only made him want more.

He was behaving badly, and he knew it. This woman wasn't what he was looking for. The problem was that he could no longer remember why.

Her blouse was made of a smooth, slinky material through which he could feel the texture of her skin and the muscles in her back as she tightened her arms around him. He stroked his hand up and down, learning her shape.

It was when she made that little sound deep in her throat again that he knew he was in trouble.

Subconsciously he'd been waiting for the tiny moan, determined to hear it and feel it again, knowing it was proof that she was as affected as he was.

And just what did he intend to do with this knowledge? Hayley was emotionally vulnerable and he had no business taking advantage of her.

Justin prided himself on being an honorable, decent man.

Kissing her was not honorable, and currently bordered on indecent.

He was taking advantage of an emotionally vulnerable woman.

The emotionally vulnerable woman squeezed his butt.

Justin's knees nearly buckled, and with a gasp he broke the kiss. "You, ah..."

She smiled. "Yes I did."

He looked into her eyes and saw the ruin of his master plan.

But drawing on the strength of experience hardened by fourteen years of denial, Justin willed a cool smile and a cooler response. "I thought so. Well, good night."

How he managed to force himself to close the door instead of grabbing her again, he never knew. But once the door was shut and he heard hers click, as well, he leaned his forehead against the painted wood.

He hurt. He ached. He wanted.

He'd been bamboozled by freckles and a pretty smile—that's what had happened. Smiles and freckles weren't supposed to pack such a wallop.

Kissing her the first time was where he'd gone wrong, Justin thought, his head still against his connecting door. No, not cleaning up that detergent was the mistake.

If he'd cleaned up the detergent, then Ross would be here now. Ross would have been the one kissing her. Justin wouldn't even have met her.

He never would have seen her smile or known how her mouth tasted or how her body felt against his or heard the little sound that she made deep in the back of her throat.

But Ross might have.

An overwhelming, baffling and totally unreasonable surge of jealousy spurted through him.

What had this woman done to him?

Hayley's door opened again and she knocked, forcing Justin to endure another hormonal attack. Cautiously he opened his door.

"Justin?"

"Yes?" His voice sounded like sandpaper.

"I have to know.... Was that a pity kiss?"

Lie. Tell her it was. Better to hurt her now than hurt her later. Lie before it's too late. He stared at her, at her wide eyes, the proud tilt to her chin and those sneaky freckles, doing a mocking dance across her nose.

"No," he admitted.

"I didn't think so." She smiled. "Night."

And she shut the door.

4

"OKAY, KIDS, let's see some enthusiasm!"

"I don't feel enthusiastic about beer at ten o'clock in the morning," Justin said, staring into the oversize stein.

Hayley cast a look at the photographer, brochure designer, bridal fair representative, the store manager of the boutique that had donated clothes for the his-and-hers trousseaux, her mother, sisters and the beaming proprietor of the trendy Beale Street nightclub where they were having their picture taken in a "natural" setting, and hoisted her beer. "I do." And she proceeded to demonstrate by downing a third of her mug.

The photographer snapped her picture. "Fabulous, Hayley. Now, Sloane, try to look less disapproving and more with it."

"Of course he disapproves," Lola said from beyond camera range. "A lady drinking beer." She shuddered.

"It's imported, Mama," Hayley said.

"Sure—from Colorado," Justin murmured.

Hayley drank more, even though they hadn't set up the next picture.

"Careful," he said. "We've got two more bar stops before lunch."

Hayley gazed directly at him. "I'm counting on it."

For a free wedding, Hayley was certainly working hard. She'd already changed clothes three times since eight o'clock this morning, but this was her first beer. It wasn't going to be her last.

In addition to several large prizes, Hayley's wedding had consisted of many modest donations, and each was acknowledged in the brochure. For instance, this little nightspot had donated dinner for two, valued at twenty-five dollars. That meant it would be combined with a modeling session and entitled to a quarter-page ad in the brochure, but nothing on the video.

In contrast, Betty's Bridal Barn had donated the wedding dress. Hayley and Sloane would appear on the cover of the brochure and in the video, and Betty's Bridal Barn would be the featured exhibitor at the next Memphis Bridal Fair.

The wedding dress. Hayley silently moaned, and downed the rest of her beer. She'd need several more to be able to deal with that dress.

"*Hayley*, dear," her mother cautioned.

"It's not like I drank it straight out of the bottle, Mama."

"I should hope not."

Mrs. Pederson, the bridal fair representative, clapped her hands. "Okay, people, listen up. Hayley, put on the black floral, and we'll go ring shopping."

Hayley desperately wished for another beer.

She looked at Justin, who eyed her warily.

He'd eyed her warily ever since she'd smiled at him this morning.

Well, did he think he could just go around kissing

women until they melted like chocolate in the hot sun, and *not* expect them to smile at him?

She propped her elbow on the table, leaned her chin on her knuckles and whispered, "Don't worry. I know it's all fake."

"Do you? We're talking diamonds here."

"No, we're not. We're talking kisses."

"Are we?"

He looked so unnerved that Hayley laughed, though inside she was depressed.

Sometime during the night, between the time she finally went to sleep and the time she stood in front of the closet in her suite at the Peabody and wondered what to wear, she'd realized that Justin was the only man she'd met in the past several years whom she could visualize marrying. She didn't think his appeal was solely due to the two kisses they'd shared, though she'd have to experience more kisses to be absolutely certain.

She had to keep reminding herself that she really didn't know him, even though she felt as if she did. Her feelings were all jumbled with him. It was probably because she was doing everything backward— planning a wedding with a near stranger when she'd never even discussed the idea with other men.

Justin managed a strained laugh and pasted a smile over his uneasiness. "I thought we were talking diamonds."

"That would be great, too." She didn't have to force a relaxed, frankly longing smile. Anyone seeing it would think it was merely a look exchanged between a bride and her groom.

Only Hayley knew it wasn't acting.

Justin looked green—maybe he suspected she wasn't acting, either. No, of course he didn't suspect. The green must have come from the sun shining through the stained-glass window sign.

"Hayley?" Her sisters beckoned.

Why were they hanging around anyway? Hayley grumbled to herself. They didn't have to show up until the bridesmaids' luncheon at noon.

"We're going shopping," Gloria announced. "When I told Ms. Winfield how much I adored this little black dress of yours, she offered Laura Jane and me discounts at her store. Wasn't that just precious of her?"

"Yes, it was." Hayley bestowed a beaming smile on Ms. Winfield, grateful to be spared the presence of her sisters during the selection of the ring.

It was bad enough that her mother would be there. Not only would Lola equate the size of the diamond Justin selected with the size of Sloane's affection and the quality with the quality of his upbringing, she would use the stone to gauge their future solidarity as a couple and the social standing to which they might aspire.

The engagement ring was fraught with symbolism. She knew her mother had been very concerned that Sloane hadn't given Hayley one yet.

She changed into the black dress in the ladies' room of the bar. This whole exercise was academic. She couldn't afford a diamond ring, even at thirty percent off. Or fifty.

She needed a new watchband. Maybe she'd use her thirty-percent-off coupon for that.

The staff at Robertson's Fine Jewelry was waiting for them. Crystal vases with fresh roses sat on the counters where spotlights made the rings sparkle.

The bridal fair people had made Justin change clothes, too, and he now wore a sport coat over a white open-throated shirt. He stood by her as they watched the preparations, his hand lightly resting on the small of her back.

The perfect fiancé.

"What? No panic attack at the sight of all these engagement rings?" she murmured under her breath.

As he usually did when she spoke softly, Justin bent his head down before responding.

Hayley had taken to murmuring quite a bit lately.

"I'm not the one who's going to be stuck with the bill."

"Not this time."

"Not for a long time," he stressed.

Justin had alluded to his desire to remain a bachelor before. "What have you got against marriage, anyway?" she asked.

"Not a thing—when the time is right. And the time won't be right for at least two more years."

"Why two years?"

"Because I've promised myself two years of fun and games before I turn respectable."

"Don't look now, but you *are* respectable."

"Yeah, I know." He grimaced. "I'm working on that."

Did all men her age think this way? If so, no wonder she couldn't find a groom. They were all in their irresponsible phases. "So how do you know you'll be ready for marriage in two years?"

"I don't. What I'm saying is that I won't be ready *before* then."

"What if you meet somebody?"

Justin chuckled. "That's the plan. I want to meet lots of somebodies."

"I mean the *right* somebody." *Like, say, me.*

He shrugged. "Then she'll have to be patient."

"While you play around?"

"She can play around, too."

Hayley gaped. She couldn't tell if he was serious, or practicing his irresponsibility. His grin widened and her eyes narrowed. "Just for that, I'm going to pick the smallest diamond Robertson's has got mounted and tell Mama that's the one you've given me."

"You do that, and I'll have a five-carat ring sized and engraved before you can say 'ten-percent restocking fee.'"

"Sloane? Hayley?" Ms. Pederson beckoned. "Mr. Robertson, himself, is going to help you."

It was Hayley's turn to paste on a fake smile.

As the camera people set up the lights, Hayley's mother herded the extra sales staff and bridal fair personnel away from the rings. "These young people have an important decision to make. After all, they're choosing more than a piece of mere jewelry."

With that, Lola draped herself against the display case featuring rings of less than a carat, fixing her future son-in-law with a gaze that implied those would be of no interest to him. Mr. Robertson headed hopefully toward the other end housing the rings with larger stones.

Hayley hesitated, finding she was curious to see what Justin would do. She looked up at him.

He slipped his arm around her waist. "If I were buying a ring today, naturally I'd select from your loose stones," he said to Mr. Robertson. "But I'd planned to give my wife the ring left to me by my aunt."

"I thought your parents were only children," Lola said.

"She was my great-aunt, actually," Justin smoothly improvised. "But I called her Aunt. Unfortunately I haven't had the opportunity to retrieve the ring from the safety deposit box and have it cleaned and the setting checked." He smiled down at Hayley. "I'm sure Hayley will be happy to model any ring you'd care to feature in your advertising."

An heirloom. Even her mother couldn't object to an heirloom. How very clever he was. She never would have known it after all the nonsense he'd spouted about becoming irresponsible.

"Have you already selected the wedding bands, then?" asked a visibly disappointed Mr. Robertson.

Even with the coupon, he would have made money on the sale of an engagement ring, as well as getting credit for a donation.

"It will be difficult to choose wedding rings without

seeing the engagement ring next to them," Hayley said. "I might have to return them."

"Return your wedding rings after the ceremony?" Lola sounded scandalized. Hayley knew she wouldn't get away without purchasing wedding rings.

"May I suggest something simple?" Mr. Robertson unlocked a display case and brought out a black velvet tray of rings. "A band of diamonds, perhaps?"

In your dreams, buddy.

"Hayley, Sloane, could we get a picture of you two looking at the rings with Mr. Robertson? We have a noon luncheon scheduled." Ms. Pederson positioned them in front of the glittering tray and pulled Lola out of the way.

"Hayley, those look real sweet," Lola called.

"Sweet" meant not big enough. *Stunning* was the word Lola hoped to say.

Hayley didn't like the rings anyway. They were too frilly, too ornate. Too not her.

"Would you show us that tray, please?" Justin pointed. He looked at Hayley assessingly. "You look like a gold person to me."

Hayley nodded as Mr. Robertson brought out the tray of gold bands and silently placed them on the counter.

"There is strength in simplicity," Justin said. "And the statement made by a solid gold band is a powerful one." His fingers hovered over the tray, bypassing the carved and etched bands, the chunky nugget bands and the multicolored bands to select a set of flat, polished circles of gold, not too thin and not too wide.

Exactly the ones Hayley would have picked. "They're perfect," she said, smiling up at him. Their eyes met and she momentarily forgot that this was all just pretend.

She was reminded when the camera flashed.

"Perfect!" shouted the brochure lady. "You just can't fake a look like that."

"Little does she know," Justin said.

"Yeah," Hayley agreed hollowly.

HAYLEY WAS REUNITED with her sisters at the brides-maids' luncheon. It was lavishly elegant with bouquets of fresh flowers and corsages for the women. The food was exquisite, the champagne flowing—and when the necessary pictures had been taken, the photographer and the others also ate lunch.

The bill was horrendous.

Hayley was discovering that she couldn't afford her "free" wedding.

As planned, Justin excused himself to use the telephone, then returned with a worried look.

"Sloane, is everything all right?" Lola asked before Hayley could.

"The El Baharis are insisting on a meeting next week," he said. "I should be there."

"Well, that's just plain impossible." Lola pooh-poohed the thought. "You'll be on your honeymoon cruise."

Justin rubbed his jaw. "We may have to postpone the honeymoon."

"Just—" Hayley nearly slipped. "Just tell them to re-schedule their meeting."

"You don't tell the El Bahari royalty when to call a meeting," Justin snapped.

"And you don't ask a bride to postpone her honeymoon," Laura Jane declared, standing up for her sister.

"*My* husband wouldn't have even considered it," added Gloria with one of her sultry looks.

"Your husband wasn't working overseas," Hayley said.

"Well, if he had been, he certainly wouldn't have been able to stay away for long."

"Unfortunately, my schedule isn't that flexible," Justin said.

Lola sent a secretive glance toward Hayley. "You may find that after the wedding, you'll desire to make it more flexible."

"Desire has nothing to do with it," Justin replied.

"Desire has *everything* to do with it."

If Hayley could get through the next two days without strangling someone—especially herself—then she ought to register at Lawrence Taylor's acting and modeling studio, because she obviously had great untapped acting talent. She put her hand on Justin's arm and a pouting expression on her face. "Sloane, are you sure you have to postpone the honeymoon?"

Justin smiled a smile that was obviously meant to appear conciliatory. "Actually, it wouldn't be postponing as much as shortening it."

"How short?" Hayley asked.

"I should leave Monday or Tuesday."

Boy, he was good. Hayley looked at the stunned

faces of her mother and sisters, and pasted on a shocked expression, as well.

Lola recovered first. "That's...that's not to be considered. That's..."

"Sloane and I will discuss this later," Hayley informed her. "In private."

"There shouldn't be anything to discuss," Lola said with a look that told Hayley she was to stand her ground.

Hayley sent her a bravely determined smile back.

This acting stuff was fun.

THIS ACTING BUSINESS was not fun at all.

"You want us to wear *what?*" Hayley and Justin were now at the lingerie store where she and her mother had purchased the rainbow of love. Because it was the day before Valentine's Day, the store was crowded as shoppers—mostly men—decimated the red and white displays.

Everyone from her sisters to the store manager thought it would be cute to have Hayley wear men's pajama tops and Sloane wear the bottoms as they posed in the furniture store that had donated a bedroom set.

"Oh, come on. It'll be so cute," the brochure lady wheedled.

After a glance at Justin's impassive face, Hayley sent a questioning look to her mother. Her sisters were busy adding to their own rainbows of love. Hayley noticed that they both bought black.

"Silk pajamas are more modest than some of the

other selections," Lola pointed out, gesturing to a filmy white negligee.

"You'll be in the bed," Ms. Pederson added.

Oh, terrific.

And was Justin helping? Of course not.

"I don't mind," he said.

"Yes, you do," Hayley said.

He held the pajama top up to her. "No, I don't."

He grinned, a lazy, molten grin, and Hayley's mouth went dry.

"It's settled, then," Ms. Pederson announced.

As soon as Hayley emerged from the furniture store rest room, Justin knew he was going to pay, and pay dearly for teasing her.

He hadn't liked looking like a jerk about the honeymoon, even though Sloane was the jerk. But to these people, *he* was Sloane, and it rankled. So he'd agreed to the "pajama games," though he could tell Hayley wasn't comfortable with the idea.

And now he was paying.

After tossing her hair over her shoulder, Hayley walked barefooted toward him, wearing the top half of the cherry red silk pajamas to which he wore the bottom half.

She self-consciously pushed up the too-long sleeves and pulled up the shoulder, which had a tendency to slither to one side.

She looked...cute, in a dangerously marriageable way. Ross's exact words. Except when the shoulder slipped, and then she just looked sexy.

Every male in the place was watching her and she didn't even notice. The camera guy had nearly dropped his camera. *Hurry up and get over here, Hayley.*

The hem rippled against the top of her thighs as she walked.

She had legs.

He'd known she had legs, but he hadn't known she had *those* legs.

HER KNEES WERE SHAKING.

Please let me make it over to the bed without falling.

Hayley tried to draw a breath and found that her lungs didn't fit her chest anymore.

Every woman in the entire bridal fair retinue, including Hayley's mother, was staring at Justin—or Sloane.

If they hadn't before, every woman in the entire bridal fair retinue now envied Hayley.

Laura Jane had to physically restrain Gloria. Lola fanned herself with her pocketbook.

Ms. Pederson repositioned the camera for a close-up. The brochure lady found an excuse to take light readings right next to him.

Justin and his casually muscled chest, his glorious shoulders and flat stomach, appeared oblivious to all.

Single women of Memphis, watch out.

Hayley was jealous of these legions of women Justin planned to date. Why wouldn't he date her?

Because he didn't want to date just one woman, that's why, and she wasn't going to humiliate herself by waiting around while he played the field.

He'd been depressingly clear and up-front about his intentions.

Hayley had another day to make him regret those intentions. It might not be impossible, she thought. He was watching her, his blue eyes following her every movement.

It would help if she knew what he was thinking.

SURELY SHE HAD on underwear.

Yes, but what sort of underwear?

Lacy underwear, skimpy underwear, see-through underwear. Underwear with hearts cut out in interesting places. Underwear he couldn't figure out. After thirty minutes in a lingerie shop, he'd seen it all.

He didn't want to think about underwear, specifically about Hayley in underwear, but it was better than thinking about her in bed, which was where they'd be mere moments from now.

"Where's the breakfast tray?" The woman from the advertising agency producing the brochure—Emily? Emma?—gestured to the store manager, one of the men who'd been ogling Hayley.

She reached them, smiled a quick little smile and tucked her hair behind her ear. She was nervous.

He drew his arm around her waist in a protective gesture that was more automatic than acting.

She had on underwear.

But not much.

BREATHE.

His hand burned where it skimmed her waist,

dipped below, then curved back up.

Try to act natural.

What was natural about being dressed in skimpy pj's in the display window of a furniture store with her sisters, her mother and a camera crew looking on?

Not to mention the gorgeous, half-naked man with his arm around her.

There was, unfortunately, nothing natural about that, either.

"Okay, you two, get in the bed and we'll arrange the tray."

Justin lifted the comforter of the overly decorated bed. Hayley shoved a few dozen pillows aside and slid in all the way to the far side.

Justin climbed in after her, leaving an entire continent between them.

"Oh, come on. Cuddle up!"

Hayley scooted toward the middle at the same time Justin did. They collided in a wave of cotton and silk.

"Perfect. Let's see if the tray will fit over both of you." The brochure lady tried to balance a breakfast tray with empty dishes and some fake croissants. "Can you get closer?"

They were supposed to be two people in love—two people in love who'd been apart for months—two people in love who were getting married in twenty-four hours.

They should be acting like they couldn't keep their hands off each other, not like they'd just met.

The problem here, Hayley thought as she slid closer

to Justin and felt his thigh press against hers, was that *they* knew they'd just met. They should be feeling awkward with the forced intimacy, but they'd also shared a couple of blockbuster kisses with the result that Hayley was having a really, really hard time not running her hands and mouth all over him.

To make this look good for her mother and sisters, she ought to look like she was enjoying herself more, shouldn't she?

"There." The brochure lady wedged the tray over their legs. "It just fits."

"They look crowded," Ms. Pederson said. "But whatever you do, don't cover up his chest."

"I wouldn't dream of it." The brochure lady looked flushed.

"Here." Justin flashed a smile at Ms. Pederson, at the same time maneuvering his arm around Hayley. "How's that?"

"Great," Ms. Pederson said with an envious smile.

It's better than great. It's fabulous. Wonderful. Life altering. Hayley sighed and settled against him, her head resting on his shoulder.

This felt way too good. She inhaled a familiar scent—they'd used the same soap last night at the hotel, but it smelled a little different on Justin than it did on her.

He was warm, he was solid, he smelled good, and he was running his fingers lightly against her arm.

Did he know? Was it on purpose? Was he acting?

Did it matter?

The camera lights came on and the furniture store's

display designer fussed with the comforter and pillows, arranging them around Hayley and Justin.

"Hon, can you move your head just a smidge lower?" the designer asked. "That way, the carving in the headboard will show."

No problem, Hayley thought.

It was warm under the comforter and lights. Justin's chest took on a sheen.

Hayley blew softly and he flinched, his thigh hardening against hers.

"What was that for?" he asked.

For heaven's sake, there was an acre of muscled male chest right in front of her face. What was a girl to do? "You looked hot."

"I am—and I don't need more heat from you."

"Why, Ju—Sloane. Are you saying I make you hot?" Without raising her head she looked up, feeling his skin beneath her cheek.

He blinked down at her, and she knew he was trying to figure out whether she was talking to him or to Sloane. Trying to figure out how she wanted him to respond.

Hayley knew exactly how she wanted him to respond and it wasn't appropriate for this situation *at all.*

And according to Justin and his two-year-plan, it wouldn't be appropriate anytime soon.

He continued to look at her, his expression unreadable, but before he could answer, the camera clicked. The whine of the auto advance drowned out the whispers of the people gathered around watching the photo shoot.

"Hayley, now feed Sloane the croissant."

"It's plastic." Justin picked it up and dropped it back onto the plate where it bounced.

"I don't expect you to eat it." The brochure lady laughed as though Justin had been terribly witty. "We're just pretending."

"Are we?" Justin glanced down at Hayley.

"Of course we are," she said, because that's what he wanted to hear. Sitting up, she took the croissant and held it to his mouth. "Why wouldn't we be?"

5

JUSTIN STOOD in the dressing room of the tuxedo rental shop and stared at his vaguely old-fashioned reflection.

Posing for that last set of pictures had been unsettling. Hayley, all warm, soft and pressed against him in bed, was not something he was going to forget anytime soon. For his peace of mind, he should forget, but his body wasn't clear on the concept of pretend.

Frankly, he wasn't sure Hayley was, either.

What had begun as an impulsive gesture to help Ross had become a serious threat to his own master plan. Specifically, Hayley was the threat.

The more Justin was around her, the more he realized how difficult it would be to walk away from her tomorrow. And if he didn't walk away tomorrow, he might not be able to walk away at all.

Bad. Very bad.

But he was going to walk away tomorrow, so what was the problem?

Not wanting to walk away might be the problem. All this wedding stuff clouded his brain. Weddings meant commitment and responsibility, so naturally he thought in those terms when Hayley was around.

Tonight, what he ought to do was get her away from

her mother, the rest of the wedding people—particularly that one barracuda sister of hers—and go somewhere where they could be themselves. Then he'd see if Hayley was flirting for real, or for fake.

HAYLEY HATED HOOPS. She hated her wedding dress. She hated her hat and the stupid parasol. And she hated pink.

It was February, and though the weather was mild, they were outdoors on the grounds of the Mallory-Neely house, a Victorian mansion, and a chill was in the air.

The photographer had wanted the late-afternoon light. Betty's Bridal Barn had wanted to showcase their "Tara" collection, and Hayley's mother was thrilled with the full-skirted antebellum dresses. Hayley's sisters didn't mind, since they weren't paying for the dresses, and would get gorgeous new costumes for those occasions when they were called upon to be old-fashioned Southern belles. Besides, the pink velvet really was their color.

Hayley looked like the top of a vanilla ice cream cone and felt about as cold.

At least Justin got to wear a jacket. With the off-the-shoulder dress, she was wearing mostly goose bumps.

He looked like Rhett Butler. Rhett Butler types had never appealed to Hayley before, but she had to admit that the outfit lent Justin a certain raffish charm.

Ahh! She was even beginning to think like her mother.

Hayley billowed over to Justin. "The South shall rise again, huh?"

He smiled. "You look very nice."

"*Nice?* I look nice?" She groaned. "The kiss of death."

He waved in an up-and-down gesture. "It doesn't seem to be your usual style."

How did he know? She remembered how he'd picked the ring she would have picked for herself. "Well, Mama liked it. I know, I know. Don't say it."

"Then I won't." Justin pushed the flaps of his coat aside and shoved his hands into his pockets, looking very nineteenth century as he did so. "Did you see a dress you liked?"

Hayley nodded. "It was long and simple with a band of pearls at the neck and waist."

"So why didn't you get it?"

"Mama said it didn't have enough presence for a big wedding."

They both looked over to the porch where Lola fussed with the bows on the backs of Gloria's and Laura Jane's dresses. Hayley herself had been adamant about not wearing a bow. She'd won that point at least.

"Sloane, Hayley!" The tireless brochure lady beckoned to them. "Over here!"

They started walking to the tree where the cameraman was setting up. "I can't help comparing this outfit to the last one you wore," Justin said.

Hayley was trying to watch the hem of her dress and keep it from snagging on the dried grass. The problem was that she couldn't *see* the hem of her dress. She was probably shedding crystal beads right and left, too. "The black dress?"

"No, the pajama top."

She looked up at him. No one was around to hear them, so he wasn't being Sloane at the moment. And that meant the look he was giving her wasn't Sloane's, either.

"Men's pajama tops are a good look for you," he said.

Only if you're wearing the bottoms. "You did wonders for the bottoms yourself. The women of Memphis will be so grateful."

He grinned, and Hayley's heart beat a little faster— the silly thing. It shouldn't beat for him—that was a good way to get broken.

They got to the tree in time to hear the tail end of a disagreement between the brochure lady and Betty, of Betty's Bridal Barn.

"The picture should be full-length," stated Betty. "Otherwise, the whole dress won't show."

"But the camera would be so far away that the details would be lost," the brochure lady told her.

"But this will be the *cover.* Shouldn't you get a better camera?"

"This is the fourth year we've produced the bridal fair brochure and there have never been any complaints."

"Ladies," Ms. Pederson interrupted. "We're losing the light. Hayley?" She pulled her to the tree. "Now lean against the trunk—"

"She'll get her dress dirty!" Lola said. "She's getting married in it tomorrow."

Ms. Pederson brushed at the tree trunk. The brochure lady positioned Hayley's hands and arms.

"And now, Sloane, can you kneel on one knee?"

"He'll get grass stains on his knee," Lola pointed out. She got a white handkerchief out of her purse and gave it to Justin.

He folded it into a square and knelt. When he gazed up at Hayley, his eyes were particularly blue in the late-afternoon light.

He looked like he was proposing, and Hayley's wayward heart thudded again. She even felt tiny and feminine in the dress.

The camera whirred.

Dozens more shots were taken, featuring Hayley and her sisters, Hayley and Sloane, and everyone together.

And then...

"Okay, you two, last one!" Even Ms. Pederson seemed wilted after the hectic day. "Kiss for the camera!"

No. Not when she was frazzled and tired and vulnerable. Not in front of her mother and her sisters and the cameraman.

Hayley could barely hold herself together as it was. She'd deflected nudgings, arch looks and pointed remarks all day from her mother, sisters, Ms. Pederson and the brochure lady. She'd changed clothes in tiny rest rooms and she'd drunk beer at ten o'clock this morning.

She wanted to fill up the bathtub and soak.

She did not want to kiss Justin pretending to be Sloane. She wanted to kiss Justin. Better yet, she wanted to lean on him and feel his arms around her.

He stepped toward her and took both her hands in his. "Long day?" he murmured and brought her hands to his lips.

The romantics in the group, Hayley's mother among them, aahed.

Hayley nodded and Justin kissed her forehead. It looked like a tender gesture between lovers.

The camera went crazy.

Hayley wanted to melt into his arms, have him sweep her off her feet and carry her up the staircase. Any staircase. Even an escalator.

Then he cradled her head with his hands and kissed her gently on the mouth.

And Hayley's heart went crazy.

This was nothing like their other two kisses. This was a gentle, nurturing kiss.

This was a kiss from Justin.

HAYLEY NEEDED TIME to give herself a major reality check. Pleading fatigue, she shooed her mother and sisters away, even though she knew they wanted to stay in the suite and talk.

"But, Hayley, won't you need help getting out of your dress?"

"If you'll just unbutton me, Mama, I'll be okay." She gave her mother a tired smile that was entirely genuine, turned around and lifted her hair.

"It's so strange. The last of my babies is getting married." Lola worked at the tiny pearl buttons that ran to the waist of Hayley's dress. "And after all these years of mothering, I'm going back to daughtering."

Hayley couldn't see her mother's expression. "Are you happy or sad, Mama?"

"I'm both. After all, this is a big change for me, too," Lola confided, "but I'm mostly happy. Oh, and I didn't get a chance to tell you, but the real-estate agent called, and I've had an offer on the house. I can't believe it happened this weekend of all weekends, but I've made a counteroffer and if it's taken, then I'll start looking at properties in Sun City as soon as things settle down after the wedding."

Her mother sounded eager. And happy. Hayley exhaled.

"Was the corset tied too tight at the waist? We don't want you fainting tomorrow."

Hayley mustered a smile as she turned around. "I'm fine." She kissed her mother on the cheek. "I just need some sleep."

After closing the door behind Lola, Hayley kicked off her dirt-stained pumps and collapsed on the bed. Her hoops and skirt popped up, blocking her view of the room.

She was alone and no longer had to pretend. The relief hit her all at once and she closed her eyes. One more day. One more day until everyone was happy. And Hayley would be happy, too, though her happiness would stem more from relief than joy.

It's worth it, she told herself. *It's all worth it.* And

every time she doubted it, she had only to remember how her mother had enjoyed today—had enjoyed planning the wedding of her dreams. The fact that it was Lola's dream didn't bother Hayley. She preferred it, knowing that she'd have more bargaining power when she planned her real wedding. As a second-time bride, she'd have earned the right to simplicity.

She was tired but she wasn't sleepy. Maybe she could take that hot bath and veg out in front of the TV.

Standing, Hayley carefully pulled the heavy dress over her head, laying the bodice on the bed and backing out of the rest of the dress. Without the hoops to hold it out, the length extended to the floor and beyond.

Other than a few dark smudges on the lining, the dress appeared to have survived the outdoor picture-taking. Hayley hung it on a padded hanger and pulled on the ribbons tying her hoops in place.

The bow loops had worked their way out, leaving a small, hard ribbon knot in back. No matter how Hayley picked at it, she couldn't work it loose. She tried turning the hoops around, but the ties were threaded through casing in the corset.

Great. Swell. Fabulous.

Her arms ached, so she shook them and tried again, this time standing in front of the full-length mirror and using the point of an ink pen. The knot turned blue, but didn't budge. What was she going to do? Cut herself out?

Muted voices sounded through the connecting door

to Justin's suite. He'd turned on the twenty-four-hour news channel.

Maybe he could help her. She grabbed for the terrycloth robe, then stopped. It would get in the way and she was more than adequately covered. The corset was made to match the wedding gown and was nearly as elaborate, with beading and lace at the top.

The entire thing was completely opaque and no more immodest than a strapless dress. The only reason Hayley hesitated at all was because of the way the clever boning in the garment enhanced her cleavage.

Normally Hayley didn't have cleavage and had never worn miracle, incredible or wonderful bustenhancing bras because she thought there wasn't enough to enhance.

An expensive garment, custom fitted by an expert, made all the difference. She looked feminine and womanly, just short of voluptuous.

She hitched the bodice higher. Well, how about that? There was voluptuous. Who'd have thought it? Hayley shook herself back to womanly. She couldn't ask for Justin's help looking voluptuous. It would be tacky.

She opened her door just wide enough to knock on his. "Justin?"

"Hang on." He turned down the TV and opened his side.

He'd obviously just pulled a T-shirt over his head and was still tugging the bottom into place. A few quick swipes with his fingers, and his hair was more or less back in place. Hayley liked the fluffiness of it.

"What's up?"

"I need help taking off my hoops."

He froze.

"This is not a come-on. There's a knot I can't get out."

"Oh. Sure. Let me take a look."

Trying to act nonchalant, Hayley opened the door all the way.

Justin didn't move, other than to blink his eyes twice.

"The knot's back here." She turned around.

"I'll need more light."

Hayley led the way to the desk lamp. Justin tilted the shade.

"Yes, you've definitely got a knot."

"I know."

"Have you got a paper clip, or something sharp?"

"What about the pins in the sewing kit?"

"Perfect. I'll get it." Justin walked past her to the bathroom. He was straightening a safety pin as he walked back out. "What do you call that thing you're wearing?"

"The hoops?"

"No, the top part."

Hayley looked down at herself. "It's a kind of corset. It was made to go under the dress. Why?"

"It's...ah—" he swallowed "—nice."

"*Nice?*" So much for her womanly charms.

"I like nice."

"Do you?"

"I like nice a lot." He walked behind her. "More and more, now that I think about it."

"That's because you're a nice guy."

He sighed, his breath tickling her neck. She felt his fingers at her back and tingles raced up her spine.

"I guess I'm going to have to get a tattoo, or something, to rough up my image."

Hayley laughed. "Your image is just fine. You won't have any trouble on your trophy-dating hunt."

"Trophy dating?"

"A woman to look good on your arm, so other men will be impressed."

"Yeah. Sounds great."

Hayley made a disgusted sound and Justin laughed.

"Speaking of, we missed dinner. Do you want to grab a bite?" he asked.

Now that she thought about it, she *was* hungry. "Yes, but not for anything complicated."

"Burgers?"

"Exactly." She tried to look at him over her shoulder.

"Hold still...there." He pulled gently. "The ribbon is frayed. You'll have to be careful tomorrow."

"Thanks." She felt the waist of the hoops open and cool air on her lower back. Holding the edges together, she turned around in time to catch an arrested expression on Justin's face.

"Okay...well..." He backed toward the door. "I'll, uh, just..." Instead of finishing the sentence, he jabbed his thumb toward the connecting door.

"I'll knock when I'm changed," she told him.

NODDING, JUSTIN BACKED through the doorway.

And he should be grateful for the escape. Sweat beaded across his upper lip. A vision of Hayley in that underwear thing would forever be burned in his mind—that and the glimpse of her back where it dipped in above her bikini panties.

He'd almost touched her, and still wanted to—wanted to press his lips against her skin.

He had to get the image out of his mind. They were sneaking out for hamburgers, nothing special. Obviously he needed a break from this wedding stuff more than he'd thought if seeing a woman in old-fashioned underwear caused this kind of reaction.

He wondered if cold showers actually worked. Now might be a good time to find out.

THEY SNUCK OUT of the Peabody without encountering any of Hayley's relatives or wedding guests who'd started to arrive, and headed to the Blues City Café on Beale Street.

Justin wished he had a hot new car to drive Hayley in. Maybe after he bought one this summer, he'd give her a call. No, he wasn't supposed to think that way about Hayley.

He remembered her standing in the light of the desk lamp, holding the back of the hoops together.

It was hard *not* to think that way about Hayley.

By unspoken agreement, they didn't talk about the wedding, but they talked about everything else.

Justin was more liberal than Hayley expected, and she was more conservative than he'd expected.

He told her funny stories about teaching high school math. She tried to respond with funny stories about being a technical writer, but there weren't any, except the time someone had sat on the copier and included the resulting photocopy as the last page of a huge technical manual. The department supervisor had failed to remove the page and it became part of five hundred manuals that were distributed to vendors throughout the Southeast.

"Did they ever find out who did it?" Justin asked.

"No, but they found out that the supervisor wasn't proofreading the manuals all the way through before signing off on them."

"Ouch." Justin smiled.

"And you should have seen the memo that went out." Hayley pushed her French fries toward him. "Have some."

He took a couple and she asked, "What made you go to work for the IRS?"

"To get experience from the inside. Corporations love to hire ex-IRS attorneys."

"When did you decide you wanted to be a lawyer?"

"That was always the plan." He ate another French fry. "I just had to do it in steps."

He found himself telling her about his goals and Ross's part in them. She listened, and Justin uneasily felt as though he was giving her more information than he'd intended.

"How is Ross doing today?" Hayley asked.

"They apparently woke him up hourly to check on him, so when I called and woke him up, he wasn't too happy."

"I guess not."

They both laughed.

"He must be getting better," Justin said. "He's complaining about the food. Too bad we can't smuggle him in some real stuff."

They stared at each other, and Justin knew the same thought occurred to them at the same time. He saw the recognition in her eyes.

"It's late. We'll have to sneak in," Hayley said as he flagged down the waiter.

"Shift change at eleven," Justin told her.

Hayley looked at her watch. "Tell the waiter to make the burger rare."

Everything seemed brighter and funnier with Hayley along. They laughed, they hushed each other, they considered possible excuses to make to the nurses, but in the end, they simply walked into the room. A curtain was drawn around the other bed. The night-light was on and Ross's eyes were shut.

"We'd better go," Hayley whispered.

Justin held a finger to his lips, then held the bag with the hamburger under Ross's nose.

Moments later, Ross's forehead creased. "I'm hallucinating fatty, fried meat and onions."

"Bingo," Justin said.

Ross's eyes flew open. "Thank God," he said, raising the bed to a sitting position. "They told me that smelling peculiar odors was a sign of brain damage." He clutched the bag. "Come to Papa."

"Are you sure he should be eating that?" Hayley asked.

"Mmm," Ross mumbled around a mouthful of hamburger.

"He had solid food at dinner," Justin said.

"'Food' is a generous description for the gelatinous mess that appeared on my plate. Hayley, dear, I'm touched that you should visit me. Justin, this is Hayley Parrish, from the wedding project. You remember me mentioning it?"

Justin and Hayley exchanged glances.

"We've met," Justin told him.

"Of course you have. I've just introduced you." Ross beamed at them, then took another bite of hamburger.

Justin shook his head at Hayley. She responded with a withering I'm-not-stupid look. "So, when are they springing you out of here?" he asked Ross.

"I've not been able to ascertain that information. How long have I been here?"

"Since yesterday."

"And where was I before that?"

"Doing laundry," Justin answered carefully, beginning to regret the impromptu burger run.

"How plebeian." Ross polished off the last of the hamburger. "Hayley, would you pour some water for me?"

"Sure, Ross." She watched him cautiously as she did so.

"Do you...do you remember the accident?" Justin asked.

"What accident?"

"The accident where you fell and hit your head," Justin elaborated.

His expression puzzled, Ross touched the bandage. "You mean I'm not in rehab?"

Justin shook his head.

"That explains why there haven't been any arts and crafts." Ross pushed out his lower lip. "Bummer."

By now, Justin realized that Ross was not going to be released anytime soon. In fact, Justin shouldn't have broken hospital rules by visiting him. He glanced at Hayley.

She looked questioningly toward the door.

Relieved that she understood, Justin nodded imperceptibly. "Ross, we've got to get going. You need your sleep."

"Do I?"

"Yes," they told him in unison.

"Then scoot, children. Oh... Justin, walk Hayley to her car. Or better yet, take her for coffee. You know, I was thinking of introducing you two after the wedding anyway. I think you'd be good for each other."

Justin and Hayley glanced at each other, then away.

"Hayley has an intriguingly devious mind that should appeal to you, Justin."

Beside him, he heard a muffled protest.

"You follow the rules too much," Ross continued. "Even the ones you make yourself. Hayley, get him to tell you about his cockamamie plan."

"Now, wait—"

"Cockamamie," Ross continued. "Isn't that a great word? I heard one of the doctors use it. I think it's a character-defining word. And it's exactly the right word to describe Justin's plan. It's a cockamamie plan. We've all fallen on swearing too much." Ross settled back, gearing up for a soliloquy. "There's no character in swearing anymore. Used to be a well-placed 'damn' would have some impact. Not anymore. Besides, damn wouldn't work here. Justin's plan isn't a damn plan. It's a crappy plan, it's full of—"

"Okay, Ross." Justin didn't have to look at Hayley to know that she was trying not to laugh. "You've made your point."

"And cockamamie makes it even better. I like that word."

"We can tell."

Ross looked at Hayley. "Do you think Sloane would use 'cockamamie'? If so, I can work it into a conversation."

"Sloane probably just swears a lot."

"Damn," Ross said, looking disappointed.

"Okay. Well." Justin looked at Hayley. "How about some coffee, Hayley?"

"I would love coffee, Justin."

"You see?" Ross beamed. "I knew you two would hit it off. I know a great many truths now. In fact, I even find that many things previously puzzling to me are now clear." Ross wrinkled his forehead. "Are you sure I'm not in rehab?"

"Not yet," Justin muttered. "So, Hayley, how about that coffee?"

"Sounds great."

They started for the door, but Ross grabbed at Justin's jacket. "She's your type of cute, isn't she?"

Justin knew Hayley had heard. "Settle down, Ross."

"Life is short. Eat dessert first."

Ross's grin was so self-satisfied, that Justin briefly—

very briefly—wanted to add another bump to his head. He lifted his hand in farewell and hoped their visit hadn't interfered with his recovery.

Hayley was leaning against the wall outside the door. "Don't look so nervous. I know Ross's grasp of reality is a little..." She wobbled her hand back and forth.

Justin stared at her. *She's your type of cute, isn't she?* Maybe Ross's grasp of reality was just fine.

"Yoo-hoo." Hayley waved her hand in front of his face. "Relax. I'm not taking anything he said seriously."

But maybe they should.

TODAY WAS HER WEDDING day. But not really.

Hayley had showered, leaving her hair wet for the hairdresser, and had finished breakfast.

On the way back to the Peabody last night, she and Justin had agreed that Justin would interrupt her preparations with messages about the increasingly volatile situation in El Bahar, with the final showdown taking place in the lobby. That way, Justin could storm off and Hayley could run back to her room. When her mother and sisters came to comfort her, she'd insist hysterically that they go on to the *Mississippi Princess*.

In one fell swoop, both Justin and Sloane would be out of her life. Sloane—good riddance. Justin... No, she wasn't going to sit around and wait for him, hoping he'd come back to her if he didn't find anyone better. That would be demeaning, not that he'd asked her to wait, but all this talk about casual dating when she and Justin were obviously...when they...

She would *not* think about Justin and his... cockamamie plans. Hayley smiled, then used the edge of the terry-cloth robe to dab at her eyes. Why bother? She could cry if she wanted to. Swollen eyes and a red nose would lend weight to her plan to convince everyone that she and Sloane were through.

She sniffed just as she heard Justin's connecting door open. Instead of the knock she expected, there was a rustling as an envelope slid under her door.

Her name was written on the outside.

Why would Justin write her a note? He knew she was in here.

Unless… Hayley's heart pounded wildly as adrenaline spurted through her system. He must have something so horrible to say he couldn't tell her face-to-face. He must have changed his mind and was leaving.

She stared at the envelope, then scooped it up, ripping out the piece of hotel stationery.

Roses are red.
Violets are blue.
If I've got to fake a wedding
I'm glad it's with you.
Happy Valentine's Day.

J.

Hayley stared at the paper and read the words over and over. She should throw it out. If her mother ever saw it…

There was a knock on the hallway door. "Hayley? Laaaa la lalaaaaa." Gloria sang the wedding march. "The front desk says the hairdresser is here."

Drawing a shuddering breath, Hayley looked over at the white connecting door. Two fat tears rolled down her cheeks as she folded the paper into a tiny square which she placed deep in the pocket of the terry-cloth robe.

ON THE OTHER SIDE of the door, an already-dressed Justin stared at the connecting door. He heard Hayley take the envelope. He imagined her reading it and hoped it made her smile.

She had a great smile.

"WHY, SLOANE, darlin', you know you can't see Hayley before the wedding." Hayley's sister Gloria batted her eyelashes at him. "But you can see *me*."

"I need to talk with her." Justin hoped he didn't sound too stern. If Blondie let him in, he was sunk because it was too early for the argument.

"So *impatient*." She wrinkled her nose. Hayley didn't wrinkle her nose like that and she had a cuter one. "I can give her a message."

Justin hesitated for effect. "Tell her that the El Baharis are being stubborn. Tell her I'll make it up to her."

"Make what up to her?" Gloria wasn't smiling now.

"She'll know," Justin said, and raked his fingers through his hair. "I need a drink." He walked off.

"But what if Hayley has something to say to you?"

"That's why I wanted you to let me in." Justin jabbed the elevator. To his surprise, it opened immediately. How about that. Just like in the movies.

What an exit.

"I THINK my corset could be tighter. There's just gallons of room at the waist." Laura Jane swirled in front of the full-length mirror.

"Hayley, Sloane gave me a message for you." Gloria,

the fake blond sausage curls bouncing against her shoulder, hurried into the bedroom. "He said to tell you that the El Baharis are being stubborn and he'll make it up to you. Now what in the Sam Hill does that mean?"

Lola, who was being combed out, swiveled in the chair. "Hayley?"

Hayley blinked rapidly. She'd discovered this morning that, for the first time in her life, she could cry at will. "Oh, Mama!" She even managed a realistic sob.

"Hayley, love, what's wrong?"

"Oh, Mama, he's got to go back to El Bahar. I won't get my honeymooooon!" She ended on a wail as her mother enfolded her in her arms.

"Surely not," murmured Lola.

"Yes, he is. I know he is. And if he does, then I'm not going to marry him!"

There was a shocked silence in the room. Hayley sobbed, just to fill it up.

"Now, Hayley..."

"Mama, if he puts his job and those awful El Baharis ahead of me on our wedding day, then he'll always put them first. What kind of a marriage would I have?"

"But, Hayley..."

Hayley sat up and looked directly into her mother's eyes. "You were right, Mama. I have to stand firm. If I give in now, at this most important time, then I'll never be first in his life. So I'm putting my foot down, just the way you taught me."

"Hayley, I think I meant you should put your foot down *after* you're married."

"I won't have any leverage then."

"Hayley!" Gloria threw up her hands. "I saw your lingerie trousseau."

"Yeah, talk about leverage!" Laura Jane pulled at the fabric at her waist.

"Laura Jane, if that were any tighter, you'd look like a sausage!" Gloria smoothed at her own tiny waist.

Laura Jane tilted her chin up. "At least my bow doesn't bounce."

Gloria flushed. "And neither would mine if they'd used a glue gun on it the way they did yours!"

"Girls! Your sister is in distress."

Hayley sniffed distressingly.

"Well, I see that." Gloria turned to the makeup artist. "This is a *wedding*. Why didn't you use the waterproof mascara?"

"It clumps," the woman said, frowning at Hayley's face.

"Better clumping than that," Laura Jane said.

Hayley felt bad about ruining her makeup application, but Gloria *did* have a point about the waterproof mascara. The makeup artist shook a bottle, dampened a tissue and handed it to Hayley, who scrubbed at her cheeks.

"No, no. Gently dab."

Hayley dabbed and Lola lectured. "It's wise to stand firm, but in this case you may be more effective if you're extremely sweet and understanding and... loving."

Laura Jane and Gloria snickered.

"Don't be vulgar, girls. Hayley, you want Sloane to

feel bad about leaving. So bad, he'll do everything in his power to return. And, I have to admit, having a man feel that he has to make something up to you is not altogether without its rewards."

"Tangible expressions of apology are always rewarding." Gloria touched the diamond pendant below her throat.

Hayley looked at Laura Jane.

"No, no diamonds," her middle sister said. "But back home, there's a precious little Mercedes sports car parked in my garage."

"And they have all that lovely gold in the Middle East," Gloria said.

"Though gold isn't worth what it was," Lola said.

"And cars depreciate," Gloria said.

Laura Jane glared at her.

"So what are you saying? I should ask for stocks and bonds before I take him back?" Hayley asked.

"Hayley, there's no need to be crass," her mother said.

"You mean stocks and bonds are crass, but diamonds and cars aren't?"

"Well, of course!"

They exchanged one of their looks of old—the I-don't-understand-you-at-all look.

Hayley really didn't want to antagonize her mother, so she quietly lifted her face to the makeup artist. She wouldn't marry Sloane if he *were* real, and her mother wasn't going to make her.

JUSTIN CALLED Hayley's room. "Hey, how's it going?" he asked when a reluctant Gloria finally called Hayley to the phone.

"Well, call them again, Sloane!" Hayley said.

He injected a sleazy tone in his voice and asked, "So, what are you wearing?"

"I don't care what time it is there, I only know that I'm standing in my wedding dress here."

"All of it, or just the good parts?"

"I'm ready to tie the knot, but I wonder about *your* commitment."

Justin clamped his eyes shut as an image of Hayley in the hoops popped into his head. He should have behaved himself. "Who's going to help you untie it?"

"You're not the only man out there."

Justin's eyes flew open and he inhaled sharply. In his mind, the image of another man—a man with Ross's face, as a matter of fact—stood behind Hayley. This man didn't resist her bare shoulders, but nibbled on them as he worked at the knot.

And then when the knot parted... The image dissolved in a haze of red as the man bent to kiss the soft skin low on her back....

"I may not be the only man out there, but I'm the best man," Justin said.

There was a silence. "I know that," she said softly.

What had he said? What were they saying? He cleared his throat. "I'll call again in a few minutes."

"I'll be waiting to hear from you...Sloane."

Sloane? She'd called him Sloane. How could she call him Sloane?

Justin was so rattled that he missed the phone cradle

and the handset bounced on the table. Hoping they hadn't heard the noise next door, he quietly replaced the phone, then sat on the bed. He wished he could turn on the television, but he was supposed to be making an overseas call.

What if they *could* hear?

"Yes, Operator, I'd like to place a call to El Bahar." He spoke loudly and distinctly.

He waited, then shouted a few things like "My fiancée is understandably upset" and "Perhaps if you could explain the situation to the king you might find that he has a romantic streak," and then, "Have you tried bribing him?"

That Sloane was such a wimp.

GLORIA AND LAURA JANE HAD their ears pressed against the connecting door. Since the hoops in their dresses didn't allow for both to be in the near vicinity at the same time, Laura Jane stood on a chair.

"Oh, Hayley, he's trying so hard, hon," she said.

"He's talking about bribing," Gloria said below her. "I wonder how much he thinks you're worth."

"Glo-ri-a!" Lola's lips thinned, but she didn't tell her two eldest daughters to stop eavesdropping.

Hayley was having a difficult time maintaining her wounded expression, and she desperately wanted to know what Justin was saying.

She'd have to ask him...but she wouldn't be seeing him again after the final argument.

It would be soon. The hairdresser and makeup artist had left, leaving an itemized bill with the total waived.

The amount was outrageous, totally outrageous. Hayley couldn't believe that she was going to have to absorb the value of Gloria and Laura Jane's hairpieces as part of her prize and thus pay income tax on her sisters' fake hair.

She'd bought them gold bangle bracelets as their bridesmaid gift, but wished she hadn't after her mother's remark about Middle Eastern gold.

The phone rang. Hayley answered it herself.

"Guess who?"

"Yes, Sloane? What did they say?"

"That I'm the world's greatest brownnoser who doesn't deserve you."

Hayley laughed in spite of herself. "I agree." She caught the hopeful expressions on the faces of her mother and sisters and knew she had to backtrack. "So, which is it, the meeting or the honeymoon?"

"If Sloane were a real man, we wouldn't be having this conversation."

How true. "You can tell me later. It's time for us to go to the dock. The limousines are here."

"Break a leg," Justin said.

"Now, Sloane, I'm sure you don't mean that."

"Hayley—"

"I haven't changed my mind," she said, and hung up the telephone.

"Well?" three female voices demanded in unison.

She shrugged. "He's trying."

"Well, we knew that!" Laura Jane hopped off her chair, dragging it beneath her hoops.

"What haven't you changed your mind about?" Gloria asked.

"He can either postpone the wedding or the meeting, but if he chooses the wedding, then it'll be a cancellation."

"Hayley, don't be foolish. We've gone to all this trouble—"

"But I didn't think it was any trouble for you, Mama. I—I thought you enjoyed planning the wedding."

Lola waved her hands. "Oh, you know what I mean," she said, tucking her handkerchief into her purse. "The wedding isn't nearly as important as your marriage. The important part is you standing up there and saying 'I do' in front of a judge. All the rest is just window dressing."

"B-but I thought the window dressing was important to you."

Lola smiled and adjusted the sleeve on Hayley's dress. "Your happiness is important to me."

Why didn't you say that a year ago? I was happy a year ago.

"We're going down in the elevator," Gloria said. "With these dresses, all of us won't be able to fit in one car."

"I wish your daddy were here to see you," Lola said.

Though she felt a pang at the mention of her father, Hayley was glad he wasn't seeing this.

She and her mother were silent as they rode the elevator down to the lobby. Gloria and Laura Jane were standing by the fountain, apparently posing for pictures from tourists delighted to see true Southern belles.

When Hayley emerged from the elevator, she heard several gasps, murmurs, then a smattering of applause.

She felt awful. Slowly she made her way to the entrance where two white limousines waited. Any second now, she'd hear—

"Hayley!"

"Sloane!" Gloria and Laura Jane shrieked and tried to hide Hayley from his sight.

"Please—I have to talk with her!"

"It's bad luck to see the bride before the wedding!"

"I saw her yesterday when we took pictures."

"But you haven't seen her this morning," Lola said firmly.

"Hayley?"

"Mama, I'd better talk to him." Hayley stepped out from behind her sisters.

"Hay—" Justin stopped and his face changed, his expression awestruck.

She smiled shyly and he visibly swallowed. "You look beautiful," he murmured.

Hayley told herself she'd always remember the look on his face and the sound of his voice telling her she was beautiful, and in her memory, it would be Justin speaking, not Sloane.

He shook his head slightly, as if to clear it. "The king refused to postpone the meeting."

"So what are you saying?"

He took her hand and led her away from her mother and sisters. "Your hands are cold," he murmured.

"I'm nervous," she confessed. "I don't know if this is going to work or not."

"Is there something else you want me to do? I will."

She bit her lip, immediately stopping when she remembered the makeup artist spending all that time lining it. "I know you would. You've been great. This has been a huge inconvenience to you and I'll never be able to repay you."

He grinned. "This is where I say I can think of a few ways you could work off your debt, right?"

Hayley's mouth quivered. "Don't make me laugh. I'm supposed to be upset."

He still held her hand and now he squeezed it. "I'll call you later. I want to know what happens."

Drawing a deep breath, Hayley looked straight at him. "Perhaps it would be better if you didn't."

His blue eyes stared at her. "Ross will ask for all the details."

"Then tell Ross to call."

It hurt to see the understanding flood his face and his expression harden. He nodded tightly. "Ready?"

She nodded.

"You sure?"

"Of course I'm sure!" she said, raising her voice.

"Hayley, be reasonable—"

"Reasonable?" She jerked her hand out of his. "*Reasonable?* You call giving up a Caribbean cruise reasonable?"

"We'll go on another cruise."

"I want to go on *this* cruise, our *honeymoon* cruise!"

Lola hurried forward.

"It'll only be for a few weeks," Justin said.

"Unless the king schedules another meeting."

"Hayley, we can always have a honeymoon, but this is my career."

"Oh!" Hayley backed away from him. "Did you hear that, Mama?"

"Everyone in the lobby has been privy to your discussion with Sloane," Lola whispered through gritted teeth.

"We *can't* always have a honeymoon. You only have a honeymoon once. After that, it's just a trip."

Justin straightened. "I'm sorry you feel that way, but I warned you it would be difficult for me to get away in February. You insisted and this is the result. We'll have to make the best of it. Go on and get in the limousine."

Lola took her arm.

"No," Hayley said. "No, I'm not going to get into the limousine, because I'm not going to marry you."

"If that's the way you feel—"

"It is. And I'm not going to wait around until you come to your senses, either." Hayley was talking to Justin then, but she suspected he didn't know it.

"Sloane, give us a moment." Lola's face had paled until the professionally applied, dusty pink blusher stood out.

Justin backed away. Lola waited until he was out of earshot, then spoke to Hayley in a tone she'd never used with her before. "Hayley Ann, you stop your tantrum right this instant!"

"Mama!"

"That man loves you and you're throwing it all away."

"No, he doesn't love me." Genuine tears filled Hayley's eyes. "He wouldn't make me happy, Mama."

"There are many kinds of happiness, Hayley. You waited patiently for well over a year while he worked in that heathen desert, and you won't give him a few more days?"

"No." She dabbed at her eyes with their waterproof mascara, and walked over to Justin. "Last chance. It's either me, or that selfish king."

"Obviously the king isn't the only selfish one around here. Goodbye, Hayley." Justin turned on his heel and stalked past Hayley's openmouthed sisters.

With a sob, Hayley whirled around and headed for the elevators. She got as far as the fountain.

"Hayley, my love!"

She knew that voice. Abruptly Hayley stopped jogging in her hoops and whirled around once more.

There was Ross St. John, in period formal attire identical to Justin's.

"Ross!" Thank goodness, Justin had intercepted him at the doors.

"I beg your pardon?"

"Ross, what are you doing here?" Justin clapped him on the back and tried to hustle him outside.

"Excuse me, my good man, but I'm afraid you've mistaken me for someone else. I'm Sloane Devereaux."

Hayley thought she might faint.

"—'s best man!" Justin said loudly. "Ross, I didn't think you were going to be able to make it!"

"Neither did I. The rehab facility didn't want to issue me a pass."

"Ross, you always were a kidder." Justin laughed, heartily and way too loudly. "Everyone, this is my *best man*, Ross St. John."

Lola's, Gloria's and Laura Jane's eyes swiveled from Ross to Justin to Hayley.

Hayley hurried over to Justin's side and took his arm. "Ross, Sloane was so disappointed when he thought you weren't going to be able to leave El Bahar and make it in time for the wedding."

Ross looked bewildered. "Justin—"

"That's right, you got here *just in* time to be my best man."

"You mean I've been recast?"

"No. I would rather do without a best man than have anyone but you playing the role."

Ross blinked and Hayley couldn't tell if he would play along or not.

Apparently, neither could Justin. "Come on, let's get into the limousine. Guests are waiting." He pulled Ross toward the doors.

"Ju—Sloane?" Hayley stared at him. He couldn't get into the limousine!

Ignoring her, he draped an arm over Ross's shoulders. "You can tell me how things were when you left El Bahar. I've been on the phone with them all morning."

"El Bahar is a dry sandy desert with the hot winds and the sun leeching the moisture out of every living thing," Ross recited. "I work for a drilling company there."

Hayley only hoped Justin could get him to the limousine in time.

"Go with them, Hayley." Lola pushed her.

"But, Mama!"

"He's already seen you and I think the time together will do you good. Maybe his friend will convince you that Sloane really must return next week."

"It doesn't matter. I don't want to marry Sloane."

"*Hayley Ann, get into that limousine.*"

Hayley went.

She plastered a smile on her face until the door shut.

"Hayley, my dear, you look ravissimo!" Ross kissed his fingertips.

"Ravissimo?"

"Rahveesheeng." This time, his accent was French.

"Thank you." Hayley looked at Justin. Justin stared back, then rolled his eyes. What, didn't he think she looked ravishing? No, what was the word he used? *Nice.* She arched an eyebrow.

"Hayley, let me introduce you to Justin Brooks. He's the friend I was telling you about," Ross said.

Justin rubbed the space between his eyebrows. "We've met."

"Of course you have. I just introduced you." Ross looked pleased with himself.

"Ross—"

"Let me." Hayley squashed down her hoops. "When you were late meeting my family, Justin filled in as Sloane Devereaux until you got here. You didn't call, you know," she said.

"I was talking to the manager of the tuxedo rental shop. He insisted that I already had a tuxedo, which was patently ridiculous. Trying to weasel out of his prize obligations, he was. I let him know that I would never accept anything free from him again, and would tell my friends not to, either."

"I'm sure he was devastated," Justin muttered.

"He was speechless," Ross told him.

Hayley gestured to his clothing. "But he must have given you the tuxedo anyway."

"Oh, well, yes he did, but only after I said I would have my attorney contact him."

"Oh, no, Ross."

"Justin, you said I could use your name in an emergency and this was an emergency. The man wouldn't listen to reason."

Justin groaned.

"Honestly, merely showing your card miraculously cuts through the red tape. And it doesn't seem to matter that you only work with numbers."

Hayley laughed, then covered her mouth, but couldn't stop. After a second, Justin joined in.

Hayley had seen his card. In addition to announcing that he was an IRS attorney, there were words like *fraud* and *auditing* on it, too. No wonder the poor man at the tux place had capitulated.

"Well, you're here now," she said, when she could talk without giggling. "But I had to go ahead and introduce Justin to my mother and sisters as Sloane, so he'll have to be Sloane, and you can play the part of best man."

"Hmm." Ross rubbed his face where his beard used to grow. "I haven't had any rehearsal time."

Justin tensed and Hayley held out her hand. "I realize we're asking a lot of you, but you're such a good actor, I know you can do it."

"Of course I can do it.... The best man delivers a toast, does he not?"

"He would if there was an actual wedding," Justin said.

"Look at her, man. You don't think there's going to be a wedding?"

"We had a fight," Hayley said.

"But you just met."

"No, I had a fight with Sloane."

"You're getting along fine now."

"We might have another fight."

"Soon," Justin added.

"No, no. That would be overdoing it. It's never good to overplay one's part."

"We're not getting married," Justin said heavily. "There will be no toast."

"I know *you're* not getting married. She's marrying Sloane."

"I'm not marrying anybody!"

"But..." Ross gestured to her, then all around them. "I'm afraid I don't understand my motivation."

Hayley made a small sound and stared out the tinted window. Disaster. Complete and utter disaster.

"Your motivation is to stay by me, Ross. We're going

to leave the limousine at the docks and grab a taxi. That's all."

"Both of us?"

"Both of us."

"That's all?"

"That's all we've got time for."

Ross inhaled deeply enough so that his nostrils flared. "I don't believe I like being relegated to a secondary role at all."

"Then you don't have to play it." Justin tapped the glass between the driver and the passengers. "The driver can let you off and we'll tell everyone that you got food poisoning on the plane."

Hayley was impressed with his quick thinking.

The intercom crackled and the driver spoke. "Yes, sir?"

"Wait." Ross straightened his lapels. "After all, it isn't the size of the role, it's what you make of it."

THE MISSISSIPPI PRINCESS and its blue paddle wheel sparkled in the bright February sunlight. The weather was cool, without being chilly, though if it should change, there were plenty of enclosed areas on the boat. In honor of Valentine's Day and Hayley's wedding, the *Mississippi Princess*'s crew was handing out sweetheart roses to the guests.

Wearily, Hayley wondered if that was part of her prize package, as well.

White streamers fluttered in the breeze. Hayley's sisters stood at the end of a gangplank decorated with hearts, one hand anchoring their picture hats, the other battling their hoops. As the limousine drew to a stop, Lola waved at Hayley.

"Isn't she a beauty?" Ross said, his hand pressed against the glass.

It was a moment before Hayley realized he was referring to the paddle-wheel steamer and not one of her sisters.

"I've lived in Memphis all these years and I've never paddled down the Mississippi. I can't think why not."

"We'll have to plan a trip on it sometime," Justin said. "My treat. A celebration after I get my new job."

Ross turned puzzled eyes toward him.

The driver opened the door and Ross climbed out, followed by Justin, who turned and spoke to Hayley. "Do you want to make an appearance, or just take the limo back?"

"It'll be easier if I shout from the car."

"Okay." He smiled down at her. "I guess this is goodbye, then. I'll try to look mad as I leave."

"Justin?"

He raised his eyebrows.

Stay in touch, Hayley wanted to say, but knew she couldn't. "Thanks again." She crossed her fingers, then shouted, "All right, then, go to your meeting! But don't expect to find me waiting when you get back!"

"Hayley—" he shouted back, but she'd caught sight of something behind him.

"Wait." She pointed. "Look!"

Ross was scurrying up the gangplank.

"What is he *doing?*" Justin waved and ran after him. "Ross!"

Ross disappeared inside the ship.

Justin trotted back to the limo. "I've got to go get him. No telling what he'll say."

"Go on. Hurry!"

Ross's view of reality changed like a kaleidoscope's. She watched Justin sprint up the gangplank between her sisters and hoped he found Ross in time.

The driver appeared in the doorway. "Need help, ma'am?"

"No, thanks. I'm staying."

"Ma'am?"

Now Hayley's mother and sisters were stomping over to the limousine. She had been expecting them.

Lola reached her first. "Hayley, we're getting blown to bits out here. What are you doing?"

"I'm not getting out," Hayley announced. "You can come in here if you want to, but I'm going back to the Peabody."

"All of us won't fit," Gloria pointed out.

"Fine. You and Laura Jane stay and enjoy yourselves."

"Hayley Ann, am I to understand that you still plan to jilt Sloane?"

"He's not the one being jilted! After hearing what Ross had to say, Sloane was talking about leaving immediately after we land in Vicksburg! Not even staying the night, Mama. Can you imagine the humiliation? Well, I won't stand for it. I'm not marrying him."

Her mother fixed her with a stern gaze. Without moving her head, she said, "Girls, go board the boat and keep Maw Maw company while I talk with your sister." Lola climbed inside the limousine. "Sloane and his best man are already on board."

"Not for long. Now that he doesn't have to waste time with the ceremony, he can leave for El Bahar immediately." It would have been better if she could have cried right then, but worrying about whether Justin caught Ross before any damage was done distracted her.

Lola eyed her. "I have never known you to act this way before, not even when you were a little girl."

It must have been refreshing after dealing with my sisters.

But Hayley was tired of arguing. "Driver? Take us back to the Peabody, please."

"Ignore her, Driver." Lola spoke with an imperious tone that was no match for Hayley's emotional one.

Great. Her only hope now was for Justin and Ross to come out and leave in a cab. Then, and only then, would her mother admit that marriage was out of the question.

Surely she wouldn't make Hayley attend the dinner reception on the boat. That would be awful.

The purser of the *Mississippi Princess* approached the limousine. "Ladies, we're due to set sail shortly. Would you please come aboard?"

He helped Lola out of the car.

Hayley stared at the ship's entrance willing Justin to appear. He didn't.

"Mr. Worrell, my daughter has a severe case of bridal jitters. Would you try to coax her out of the car?"

Obviously Hayley and Sloane were going to have to fight in front of the guests. *Then* they could leave.

Before the purser could say anything, Hayley flashed him a cooperative smile, took a step and felt the heel of her shoe catch on her dress. *See, see? It's a sign.* Carefully she reached down and gathered the fabric out of the way. Crouching low, she crept toward the door.

"Need a hand?" he asked.

"Yes. Two aren't adequate." Hayley stepped out with one foot, then released that side of her dress and took the purser's hand. She winced as she heard the crystal beading scrape along the side of the car.

"You look very pretty, ma'am."

Lola smiled. "Yes, doesn't she look lovely?" But as they walked to the gangplank with the purser, her mother leaned close and spoke into Hayley's ear. "You mustn't overset yourself so. You're beginning to blotch."

Her mother hadn't seen anything yet.

As soon as Hayley was on board, she scanned the lobby area for Justin or Ross, but couldn't find either.

"Hayley, we're using the bridal suite to freshen up before the ceremony."

"Thanks, Mama. I'll just stay here a minute and...and breathe the fresh air."

Since the Mississippi wasn't the most fragrant of rivers, Lola regarded her suspiciously and refused to leave.

A blast from the pilothouse signaled the imminent departure of the *Mississippi Princess*.

Hayley panicked. "I can't do this!" She started for the door, but her mother grabbed hold of her dress.

"You can and you will."

"But marrying Sloane is a terrible mistake." She pulled at her dress. "Let me go. If you don't, I'll tear the dress. See if I won't."

"Is there a ship's doctor?" Lola asked the hovering purser. "My daughter might require a sedative until she is able to control her emotions."

"You're going to drug me so I'll marry Sloane?"

Running feet pounded a metallic tattoo. Justin rounded the corner, his face set. He pulled up short, chest heaving.

"Hayley." Breathing hard, he stared at her.

"You see, Mama? He's on his way to El Bahar." Hayley averted her face. "Goodbye, Sloane."

"I'm...not going to El Bahar."

Hayley jerked her head so fast, she pulled a muscle. "Maybe not this instant, but in a couple of days."

He shook his head.

Hayley stared at him until her eyeballs hurt.

"*Ross,*" he said with heavy emphasis, "convinced me that I was being a fool to even consider postponing our honeymoon."

"Oh, Hayley!" Lola clasped her hands together.

"What are you *saying?*" Hayley was in a parallel universe, that's what had happened. "The Twilight Zone" had become reality.

Justin gave her a sick smile. "I'm saying that you're absolutely right. I *shouldn't* put my career ahead of our marriage."

Ross must have hit him on the head. He was delusional. "Oh...oh, sure, you say that *now*, b-because you don't want to look bad in front of my mother."

"Hayley!" A quick glance at Lola told Hayley that Justin was looking fine in her eyes, however Hayley had been relegated to the status of a child having a tantrum instead of a woman to be pitied.

"But I know what'll happen the next time. In fact—" her voice gained assurance "—I'll bet what happened this time is that the king postponed the meeting and you're trying to get credit for standing up to him."

"Have you paged the doctor yet?" Lola asked the purser.

Justin's breathing had returned to normal and he was able to appear calm and contrite. "I'm sorry, Hayley. I've put you through so much, that I don't blame you for not believing me. But I've changed."

"You've changed, all right." Hayley knew she wasn't going to win this one. For some reason Justin had rewritten the script without telling her. "Next, you're going to announce that your name isn't even Sloane," she couldn't resist saying.

He half smiled. "I do prefer to go by Justin."

There was another blast from the horn and the door closed behind them.

Hayley and Justin—Ross, too—were stuck on the *Mississippi Princess*.

What now?

"WELL? WHAT'S YOUR PLAN?" Hayley asked. She was in the bridal suite stateroom at the top of the *Mississippi Princess*, supposedly resting and allowing her blotches to fade. Justin and Ross had climbed up to the balcony from the deck below. Ross had been lured up there with promises of a spectacular view of the paddle wheel, and a steamboat pilot's view of the Mississippi, which he was currently enjoying outside the sliding glass doors.

Justin had collapsed in a club chair in the sitting area, his feet stretched out in front of him. "My plan was damage control." He gestured toward Ross. "There's the damage, under control. For the moment."

Hayley sat in a pool of dress in the center of the bed. "So now what?"

"What do you mean, now what? Keep him amused, I guess."

"*That's* your plan?"

"Have you got a better one?"

"*No!*" Hayley's blotches weren't fading. "My plan was to go back to the Peabody! You mean you ruined my plan and you didn't have another one?"

"No, I didn't have another plan! Apparently, I'm not as devious as Ross thinks you are and can only deal with one plan at a time!"

"Which you torpedoed!"

Justin stared out the glass doors where Ross had raised his face to the sun. The wind blew his hair, showing the stitches at the back of his scalp.

Hayley looked away.

So did Justin. "When I found Ross, he was going on about how he'd introduced us, and how perfect we were for each other. He'd already referred to this as a whirlwind courtship and called me Justin." He leveled a look at her. "Your sisters were there."

Hayley gasped and felt the corset squeeze her rib cage. "What did you say?"

"Tried to make a 'just in time' joke out of it and sent him to arrange for a bottle of champagne to be delivered to each of the bridal party dinner tables. That's when I found you."

He'd done the best he could, Hayley acknowledged. "Now what?"

"I don't know. Hide out here, I guess."

Hayley stared at him in disbelief. "There is a boatload of people in the grand salon expecting a wedding!"

Justin drummed his fingers on the padded arm of the chair. "We could have another fight."

"I don't think so." Hayley's reputation would suffer enough as it was by the time her mother and sisters finished confiding in their close friends.

"Then we'll call your mother in here and tell her that we've decided not to marry."

"She's already talking drugs, Justin."

"No kidding?"

"Sedatives."

He looked out the window. Ross had taken off his jacket and had extended his arms as though embracing the view and all of Memphis. "Sedatives could be useful," Justin said.

"He's not going to do a swan dive off the railing, is he?"

"Ross can't swim."

"Do you think he remembers?"

"I don't know."

They stared at Ross. "Okay," Justin said. "Your mother wants to see a wedding, then let's show her a wedding."

For one bright and shining moment, a perfect golden moment of happiness, Hayley thought Justin was proposing.

But only for a moment. "And how are we supposed to do that?"

He looked at her in surprise. "We've got the outfits, the rings and the judge. What else do we need?"

"A license?"

"We can't get a license. My name isn't Sloane."

"I *know* that. But I never intended to set foot on this boat. The judge has no idea that there wasn't going to be a wedding. He's a real judge."

Justin smiled. "Then that's your out. We'll tell him we don't have the license with us. He'll refuse to perform the ceremony, and we'll tell your mother. Problem solved."

"Except I still won't be married."

"Okay. We were supposed to stay on the boat all the way to New Orleans anyway. Tell her we eloped there."

She thought over the new plan, finding it plausible. "That might work." Hayley smiled, feeling relieved. "Thanks."

Justin stood. "Keep an eye on Ross and I'll track down the judge."

THE JUDGE REMINDED HAYLEY of Santa Claus with a cigar.

"Forgot the license, didja? Ho, ho, ho," he chuckled, slapped his knees and gave them a stern look. "Then ya can't get married."

"We thoroughly understand your position, sir." Justin stood before him like the lawyer he was.

"No, son, don't believe you do." He adjusted his bulk in the club chair, took out his cigar, flashed a smile at Ross, then put the cigar back in his mouth before turning back to Justin and Hayley.

"Perfect," Ross mouthed. He'd been entrusted with

someone's video camera and was taping Justin and Hayley's conversation with the judge.

Hayley agreed with Justin that this was the best way to keep Ross busy and quiet. They'd destroy the tape later.

"I meant that you can't get married legally *today*. Now there was a time, early in my thirty-three-year career, when I was a stickler for the letter of the law. Didn't last long, but I'll own up to it. What I had to learn was that we have judges for a reason and it is this."

He glanced at Ross, who gave him a thumbs-up. "Things are not black and white. So this is what I'm gonna do. I'll perform the ceremony today, and you two come see me in my chambers with that license, because until I sign that license—" he paused to look sternly at both of them "—you two won't be married any more than actors in a play...and you're not to present yourselves otherwise. Agreed?"

Actors in a play. That's exactly what they were. Justin and Hayley nodded.

The judge slapped his knees once more and worked himself out of the chair. "Then let's get this show on the road. Lobsters are gettin' overcooked."

AFTER HUNDREDS OF HOURS of work, incredible expense and stress of a magnitude that Hayley never again wanted to experience, the wedding was over in ten minutes.

Pronouncing them man and wife with an exaggerated wink, the judge instructed Sloane to kiss the bride.

Hayley lifted her face and received a light, chaste peck, but knew it was Sloane kissing her, not Justin.

As the guests applauded, an amplified voice announced, "And now, Hayley and Sloane's song."

"Do we have a song?" Hayley asked.

"I guess we do now." Justin nodded toward the platform where Ross had commandeered the microphone.

The twelve-piece orchestra began to play.

"Justin...Justin, he's going to sing."

"Ross can't sing. He's taken years of lessons, but—"

Ross began to sing in a credible Elvis voice. After a ragged start, his voice smoothed and mellowed, strengthened and soared.

Everyone's attention was riveted to the platform. Goose bumps prickled on Hayley's arms. "I think the lessons worked," she whispered.

"How about that?" Justin stared at his erstwhile best man.

Did Ross have to pick "Can't Help Falling in Love" to sing? Couldn't he have picked "Blue Suede Shoes" or another snappy number? "Jailhouse Rock," maybe?

Everyone was staring at them.

At a loss, Hayley looked at Justin. He looked at her. The syrupy music flowed around them.

A corner of Justin's mouth tilted up, and he took her in his arms, no mean feat, considering her hoops, and danced her in ever-widening circles as the crowd stepped away from them.

The orchestra swelled. Ross emoted.

And Hayley dreamed.

She'd fallen in love with Justin. Improbable. Unlikely. Impractical. Based on an acquaintanceship of days. With no future at all. Foolish, foolish, foolish.

She couldn't help it, just like the song said.

The music died away, and in the tender silence that followed, Justin kissed her.

She might have had a chance to save herself if he hadn't kissed her right then, but this kiss was exactly the way she imagined a kiss of love, promises and commitment would feel. Even though he didn't love her, was making no promises and committing to nothing, she was lost.

With more than a few surreptitiously wiping their eyes, the guests laughed and applauded. At the explosion of sound, Justin jerked his head up and stared at her. He looked dazed.

"My baby!" Lola, followed closely by Hayley's sisters and grandmother, crowded around them hugging, laughing and crying. "I *knew* everything would work out!"

When others began to approach them, Lola organized everyone into a receiving line. The orchestra played background music and Hayley, with Justin at her side and Ross happily back to videotaping, greeted her guests,

Over and over they repeated the details of Sloane's background until Hayley wanted to scream.

"You are *so* lucky, Hayley," said one of the other technical writers who worked with her. The woman eyed Justin. "It's a good thing she kept you hidden."

JUSTIN HAD HEARD that comment or a variation of it more than he should have. Hayley was standing right there. She wasn't his wife, but these women didn't know that, and flirting with a married man in front of his bride was anything but appropriate.

"Once I found Hayley, I stopped looking at anybody else," he said, and smiled down at her.

Hayley smiling back at him was plenty of reward.

"Where *ever* did Hayley find you?" asked another young woman.

"Ross introduced us," he replied.

"Then *promise* me you'll introduce me to Ross," she pleaded with a laugh, her hand on his arm.

She moved on to Hayley. "Hayley, you're just the *luckiest* thing."

No one had told Justin *he* was lucky. No one had said, "You've got yourself a wonderful girl."

"She waited for me for over a year," Justin said to nobody in particular.

The woman with Hayley answered him. "Well, sugar, I'd wait for you, too."

Hayley laughed. "And people thought I was crazy."

"Like a fox," the woman said, and moved on to Lola.

Other comments drifted toward Justin. "Hayley did better than we expected," a woman with a cigarette voice told Lola.

He hoped Hayley hadn't heard, but she stood on tip-toe and quickly whispered in his ear, "Got a swelled head, yet?" Then she greeted another person.

Something else bothered Justin. Here he was, without a sole guest except Ross, and no one had commented. From other things they'd said, he knew none of these people suffered from being overly polite, so weren't they the least bit curious about the sort of man Hayley was marrying?

"My parents are dead and I have no brothers and sisters," he offered to the next couple.

"So sorry," they said. "Hayley, dear! You are so *lucky!*"

On the other hand, without people seated in the traditional way with the bride's guests on one side, groom's on the other, who would know that he didn't have anyone here? That must be it. Hey, they might actually pull this off.

He turned to Hayley, intending to say that to her, and noticed the unguarded outsider-looking-in expression on her face as she watched her mother and sisters. The same couple to whom he'd announced his lack of immediate family was now gushing to Lola. Hayley was listening, so Justin did, too.

"Lola, everyone is so envious of you. This is *the* wedding of the entire social season. No one will be able to compete. What a triumph for you and for your last daughter, too. Why, who'd have thought that Hayley... Well, we heard you'd about given up on her, and now look what she did. You must be so proud."

"We had some rough moments, but everything has turned out beautifully," Lola said with a queenly smile.

The couple made some remark about Hayley's mother moving away and Justin suddenly realized that this wasn't so much a wedding reception for Hayley as it was a goodbye party for Lola.

And just a plain party for Hayley's friends.

People filed directly from the receiving line to the buffet, washing down the expensive food with drinks from the open bar. After dancing for a chunk of the night, they'd land in Vicksburg, and be transported back to Memphis in luxurious bridal buses.

And Hayley was paying for it all. Not the full value, but the taxes. From what he'd seen, he'd guess that the cost of this entire production was more than her yearly salary. He wondered exactly what her tax bill was. In fact, he ought to examine the valuations the donating companies had assigned to their prizes and make sure the amounts weren't inflated. He could do that for her at least.

She wasn't appreciated enough, he decided, murmuring social nothings to the next clump of people. No one here appreciated the Hayley he'd come to know. They compared her to her mother and sisters and found her lacking, rather than valuing her different-ness. No, she wasn't a short, stacked blonde with big eyes. She was a taller brunette with hazel eyes and a wide smile.

He remembered seeing her in the corset she was wearing under her gown even at this moment. She was gorgeous then and gorgeous now.

Were these people blind? Why hadn't any of the males come through the line and jabbed him in the arm, or shaken his hand and told him he was lucky?

The last people in line were approaching and Justin was glad. He intended to circulate and proclaim how delighted and lucky he was to be Hayley's husband.

He wanted every man present to envy him—and to let Hayley know it.

"HEY, THERE, FRIENDS. How about a little five-card stud?" Ross waggled his eyebrows and riffled a deck of cards.

"Where's the video camera?" Justin asked. He and Hayley had eaten and were preparing to cut the wedding cake.

Ross lowered his voice and leaned forward. "I find that I stay fresher when I divide my time between acting and directing." He riffled the cards again. "Deuces and one-eyed jacks wild?"

"What are you doing?" Justin asked.

Ross bowed. "Ross St. John, riverboat gambler, at your service. Oh, and Justin...?"

"Yes?" Justin asked warily.

"When you've finished using the name Sloane, may I have it? Sloane St. John sounds more attractive to the ladies." He tipped an imaginary hat and swaggered off.

Hayley giggled.

Justin stared after him. "I'm sorry."

"What for?" she asked.

"If he hasn't already, he'll probably start a card game and win money from your friends."

She shrugged. "It doesn't bother me. Is he good at cards?"

"Who knows? I didn't think he could sing."

"It must be the bump on the head."

"Evidently." Justin led her to the cake table. "He's

exhibiting so many new talents, I hate to take him back to the hospital."

The wedding cake was a stunning example of the expertise of the chef at Cake Sculpture, the donating bakery. Hearts, doves, figures, sugar roses, columns and platforms of various heights made it look like a float in the Tournament of Roses Parade. Hayley hardly knew where to cut it. Justin pointed to the base and placed his hand over hers.

They fed each other slivers of cake. Once again, the amplified voice of Ross filled the room.

"Attention! As best man, it is my duty—nay, my pleasure—"

"Nay?" Justin muttered.

"—to offer a toast to the bride and groom." The room grew silent. Ross made certain of it. "I've known the man you call Sloane since we were in school together, and have never met a more solid and determined individual. He worked his way through college with the idea of becoming a lawyer. But he knew he wouldn't be able to afford full-time law school right away, so he taught high school math, inspiring the minds of the next generation, and went to law school at night."

Justin cringed. It was his background everyone was listening to, not Sloane's.

"They think you're an engineer who works for an oil company," Hayley whispered.

"What can I do? Ross has got a microphone. He's armed and dangerous."

Hayley laughed silently. "It doesn't matter. My mother thinks I'm married. That's all that matters."

Justin wanted to tell her she was wrong, but discovered he couldn't.

"And when he achieved his goal, he continued to work hard, determined to clear himself of debt before marrying. And marry he has to the lovely Hayley, whom I have known but a short, though sweet time, while we, er..." Ross seemed to remember the details of their situation "...er...collaborated on a recent project. When I met her, I thought of him, and the result is as you see before you." Ross raised his glass. "I give you Hayley and...and Sloane!"

"Hear, hear!" someone called out.

"The toast actually wasn't too bad," Justin said.

"Mama's probably hyperventilating to find out you're a lawyer."

Gloria marched up to the microphone, apparently deciding to perform her matron-of-honor duties and offer a toast, as well.

But Ross swiveled his hips and refused to relinquish the microphone. "And now, ladiesangenelmen, ah give ya once more, their song." He signaled the orchestra to play "Love Me Tender."

"I thought our song was 'Can't Help Falling In Love,'" Hayley said.

"We have lots of songs. Let's dance."

She felt as natural in his arms as any woman wearing hoops could.

With an unexpected surge of emotion, Justin realized that what he wanted to do was love Hayley tender, just like the song said. Unfortunately, the timing was wrong.

Hayley deserved to be married, he thought. She was just the type for life in suburbia. Not with him, though. He wasn't ready for that. He still had a long job hunt and loans to repay before he could even *think* about marriage.

But for now, for the duration of the song, she was in his arms and he could pretend.

JUSTIN WAS A BETTER ACTOR than Ross, Hayley thought as they danced together. *He's looking at me as if I'm the only woman in the world for him.*

If only it were true.

Ross finished the song, but Justin didn't seem to realize it because he still held Hayley in his arms.

"Thankya. Thankyaverymuch."

As the orchestra began to play again, Ross had another announcement in another accent. "And now, ladies and gentlemen, do you feel lucky? Join me in the *petit salon* for a friendly little game I call 'Valentine poker.' Hearts are worth double." Ross riffled his cards into the microphone and hopped off the stage.

"Thank you for dancing with me," Hayley said, since they were still swaying around the room.

"My pleasure," Justin replied.

"Hayley, sweetie, the guests are growing restless." Lola appeared beside them. "Throw your bouquet and then you and Sloane can leave."

"Leave?" Hayley blinked at her mother.

Lola dimpled. "Why, yes, darling. It's time to start your honeymoon."

8

HAYLEY AND JUSTIN STARED at the bridal suite. During the time they'd been in the grand saloon pretending to get married, the room had been transformed into a bower of romance.

The steward had unpacked all their luggage and had arranged Hayley's white negligee in the shape of a swan which swam at the foot of the bed. Apparently, their cabin steward subscribed to the "rainbow of love" theory, too.

No less than three bottles of champagne chilled in buckets of ice, and an array of hors d'oeuvres on silver trays adorned the tiny table in the sitting area next to the picture window. Fresh flowers sat on both bedside tables and fat white candles were clustered on the vanity.

"The wax is barely melted," Justin pointed out. "He must have been watching for our grand exit."

The idea of being watched made Hayley feel creepy.

The idea of being in a honeymoon suite with a man she wasn't married to wasn't reassuring, either.

In fact, it was depressing. She longed for solitude, chocolate and a hot bath.

Justin shrugged out of his jacket and hung it up in

the closet. Then he stood, hands on hips, and stared at Hayley's side. "What's all this?"

It was the rainbow of love, but she wasn't going to tell him. "My nightgowns." Even her sisters had acknowledged that in this area, Mama knew best.

Justin pushed past a short slip splashed in orange poppies with matching kimono, and withdrew a long gown. The top was stretchy peach lace and the bottom was a single layer of blush-colored chiffon. Transparent chiffon. He glanced from the gown to her, then put the garment back.

While Justin was looking at the gowns, Hayley was remembering that they were all she had to wear. She'd let her mother and sisters pack, never thinking she'd be in this situation. She longed for the terry-cloth robe, or even her favorite Mickey Mouse nightshirt.

What she had was the white peignoir. If she remembered to keep the robe pulled closed, it wasn't too bad. Four layers of heavy chiffon and some expensive lace were between Hayley and indecency with a fake husband.

Well, she couldn't stay in the hoops, could she?

Justin had wandered over to one of the ice buckets. "'Best wishes from Ross,'" he read, and laughed.

"Ross!" Hayley stared at Justin. "What is he going to do? What if he gets off in Vicksburg?"

"I'll check, and if he does get off—but remember, he's organizing a poker game—I'll wait until the buses leave, then rent a car and follow him back to the Peabody."

"That sounds like a good plan." Sighing, she kicked off her shoes. Her toes embraced the plush carpet.

"Hey, do you need help getting out of your dress?"

Hayley gave him a look.

Justin grimaced. "Please. We're past that, aren't we?"

Darn. "If you can get the buttons in the middle of my back, I can get the rest."

She turned around and pulled her hair out of the way, conscious of having done so one other time.

"I see why women back then had ladies' maids," Justin said, his fingers working the buttons and loops. "What would you have done if I hadn't been here?"

"Ripped," Hayley told him.

"Then I'm glad I'm here."

It was such a gallant thing to say, that Hayley didn't point out that if he weren't there, she wouldn't be in this situation.

"Okay," he said, after several minutes of silence filled by the rhythmic sloshing of the paddle wheel. "I'll untie the ribbons on your hoops, too."

Hayley felt the waist loosen and took her first truly deep breath in hours. "Thanks," she said, turning back around. "You can't imagine how liberating that feels."

Justin's eyes looked very blue. "I'll, uh, duck in the bathroom and give you some privacy. Knock when you're decent."

He grabbed a shirt and slacks, and disappeared into the bathroom.

Hayley maneuvered her way out of the dress, hoops and corset, and slipped on the flowing white gown.

"You can come out now," she called to Justin, and went to hang up the dress and figure out what to do with the hoops.

THAT DIDN'T TAKE LONG, Justin thought. He opened the door. "Did you know that there is a whole basket of bubble—"

He broke off. From the closet, Hayley looked inquiringly at him.

She was wearing a white outfit that revealed the shadows of her legs in the candlelight. "Is that your idea of decent?"

She looked down at herself. "You can't see through it, can you?"

"I—" Not entirely. "That's not the point."

"What is the point?"

He waved his finger. "That's a...a..."

"Peignoir," she told him calmly.

"Yes. Peignoir." He'd seen enough old movies to know that women in peignoirs were ready for romance. And he was standing in a room so crowded with romantic notions he tripped over them every time he turned around.

She looped ribbons over a padded hanger. "Would you prefer that I wear one of the others?"

He'd seen the others. Yeah, he'd like to see her in the others, especially the black one with the interesting lace insets. But he wasn't falling for that trap. "It seems dressy for the occasion."

Hayley sighed and looked away. "And what, exactly, is the occasion?"

Justin felt he was in a no-win situation. No matter what he said, it wouldn't be the right thing. "I thought we were waiting around until we could, or until *I* could, leave the boat."

"So what *is* appropriate to wear to an après faux wedding supper?"

Judging by the tone of her voice, he was headed for disaster. Better surrender now. Justin hung up his tuxedo. "I'm sorry. I don't know why I'm apologizing, but I am sorry."

"No." She touched his arm. "I apologize. My mother and sisters packed my bags and I don't have anything to lounge around in except what you see here." She ran her hands across the fluffy stuff in the closet. "The fact is, Justin, this day has been very...emotionally draining. I feel like crying. I want to cry. I *need* to cry. And I *deserve* a good cry. I'll feel much better afterward."

Justin stared at her. She seemed so matter-of-fact about it. The only female crying he was familiar with were his mother's late-night sobs of despair.

"What you should do..." she continued.

Yes, please tell me what to do.

"Is watch a movie, or eat or something."

"Watch a movie?"

"Yes." She walked toward the bathroom. "I'll try not to disturb you."

This wasn't right. He may not know what right was, but he did know this wasn't it.

"I trust there's an ample supply of tissues?"

"Hayley..." He followed in her wake.

"Don't worry, Justin."

His name sounded funny. She was already crying.

"Aw, Hayley…"

"*What?*" She spun in the doorway, her eyes bright with tears.

Yes, what? "Don't cry."

"Ooo!" She ripped half a dozen tissues out of the dispenser. "After a day—no, a *year*—like the one I've had, I'm *entitled* to cry, and nobody's going to stop meeeeee!"

Her face crumpled and he held out his arms. She shook her head and tried to close the bathroom door, but Justin wouldn't let her.

"Go *awaaaay!*"

"No."

She stared at him, hiccupped a sob and then she was in his arms.

Justin held her shaking body, feeling the same weary helplessness he felt when he was a boy and heard his mother crying late at night. Sometimes he'd get out of bed and find her—usually at the tiny kitchen table surrounded by papers he now knew were bills—and hold her, much as he was holding Hayley now.

At first his mother had tried to hide her tears, just as Hayley had done, but when he was older, she'd just cried and clung to him.

Justin didn't speak. He automatically stroked Hayley's back and hair and allowed his mind to wander, thinking over his childhood, his friendship with Ross and the extraordinary events of the past few days. He didn't think Hayley was crying over bills, though she probably should.

It was at that point that he began to think about Hayley herself. After spending hours with her mother and sisters, he thought he had a fairly good idea of her childhood. It was the ugly-duckling scenario, only, nobody had realized that Hayley had turned into a swan. But he sensed that there was love in the family, even if there wasn't acceptance.

What a wonderful mother she'd be.

The astonishing thought popped out of nowhere and it alarmed him. Okay, deep breaths.

Hayley's sobs quieted, her head heavy as his chest rose and fell. "I'm sorry," she whispered. "I know men don't like it when women cry."

"Because guys feel helpless." Justin reached around her and turned off the bathroom light, leaving the outer room illuminated by the candles and the closet light. "Let's sit down."

His arm around her, Justin urged her over to the small sofa, which he turned around so they could see the view. Lights from houses on the bank of the Mississippi made smeary reflections in the water. He found the sight restful and hoped Hayley did, as well.

"I feel better now," she said. "All the wedding stuff got to me at once. I mean, it's supposed to be the most important day of a woman's life and...and...oh, drat." She brought a tissue to her nose.

He got up and opened the bottle of champagne Ross had sent, then moved the ice bucket next to the sofa and poured two glasses, handing Hayley one. "See if this doesn't help you relax."

"Champagne is for celebrating," she said.

"So let's celebrate." Justin clinked his glass against hers. "Here's to pulling off your wedding."

With a trembly little smile that went straight to his heart, she clinked her glass against his.

"Do you want something to eat?" he asked before he said something stupid. "There's quite a spread here."

"Sure."

He brought her a plate with an assortment of elaborate little mouthfuls.

"Smoked salmon." She sighed, and popped a pink puff into her mouth. "I love smoked salmon."

Justin promptly put all the smoked salmon hors d'oeuvres on her plate and she laughed.

Her laugh made him feel as though he'd done something wonderful.

Dangerous feelings, the sort of feelings that made a man want to juggle his financial commitments.

Sipping her champagne, Hayley propped her legs on the club chair. The chiffon settled limply around them, leaving their shape clearly defined. She'd painted her toenails with an opalescent polish that changed colors in the flickering candlelight, like an oil slick in the sun.

He stared at her toes, watching the colors change from pink to purple to blue to silvery white. Maybe marriage wasn't completely out of the question....
Abruptly catching himself, Justin ate a cheese cube, then ripped a couple of grapes off a stalk.

"Those look good." Hayley casually reached over and took a grape for herself. "Do you want to try one of the salmon ones?"

"Sure." As he ate, Justin thought that, with anyone

else, the current situation would be intolerably awkward. With Hayley it was relaxing. Companionable. Lulled by the rhythmic paddle wheel, Justin imagined sitting with her, watching the lights drift by and eating wonderfully exotic food for hours. Days. Weeks. An eterni—

"Do you hear something?" Hayley asked.

Justin listened, hearing faint music over the sloshing paddle wheel. "It's coming from outside," he realized. He got up and slid open the glass door to the balcony.

The lyrics to "Big Hunk O' Love" filled the night.

"That's Ross again." Hayley grinned.

Stepping to the edge of the balcony, Justin leaned over the railing until he could see the deck below. "Yes, Elvis has returned for his second set and is apparently serenading us." Justin closed the door. "I've known Ross a long time, but I had no idea he could sing."

Hayley held out her glass and Justin refilled it. "You two make odd friends."

"That's what I told him, but we get along." Justin settled himself back on the couch. At least Hayley wasn't crying anymore. He didn't mind talking to distract her—or even listening if she wanted to talk.

"I like him, too. During the toast he gave, he said you went to school together."

"We were potluck roommates our freshmen year." Justin sipped his champagne. Not bad. Ross did know his wines, though he rarely had enough money to demonstrate his expertise. "I went to class during the day and studied at night. Ross slept during the day and went to class or plays at night. He was a theater major. Royally ticked off his father, who wants Ross to join the family business."

"Which is...?" Hayley shifted and threw the edge of her robe over her legs.

Like that covered anything.

"They sell office furniture. And the funny thing is, Ross is really good at it. He's got a knack for seeing how space can be used, and he helps people visualize it."

"I'll bet he learned how in his set-design classes."

Justin had never considered that before. "Could be." He chased an olive around the plate, then stretched over to the serving tray and speared some prosciutto and melon.

"I got the impression that Ross and his dad didn't get along." Hayley leaned her arm against the sofa back as though settling in for a long talk.

That was fine with Justin. Talking was infinitely preferable to crying. "His dad didn't handle Ross right at all. I've seen them together, and Mr. St. John doesn't understand that Ross's creativity is his strength. It's what makes him such a good salesman. They're always fighting. Ross knows how to push all the hot buttons. Anyway, he decided he wanted to be an actor and swore he'd never take a penny from his father."

"Has he?"

Justin met her eyes. "I needed a loan to go to law school, but couldn't get one because I already had huge loans from college to repay. So you know what Ross does? He goes to his father and asks for money. Listens to this big I-told-you-so lecture, but gets a potful of money and parks it in a bank, then cosigns my loan using the money as collateral. He did it for me, and I don't even know why."

"Because he's your friend."

"But...why? We're not anything alike."

Hayley ate the last of the salmon. "Do you remember the toast? He called you an inspiration. He's seen you work toward your goal and I think it encourages him to work toward his own goal, whatever it is. Also, how can you not like a guy who'll drop everything to help a friend honor his commitment?"

The shine in her eyes wasn't entirely due to leftover tears. "Hayley, don't make me out to be this noble white knight. Ross fell because *I* spilled detergent and hadn't cleaned it up yet. The whole accident was my fault."

Instead of looking disgusted, her smile widened. "How can you not like a guy who'll admit to his mistakes and try to make them right?"

HAYLEY WAS WEARING an expensive cloud of chiffon. Candlelight flickered in the room. There was champagne, fresh flowers, wonderful food, a breathtakingly romantic view and a handsome man.

So what, exactly, was wrong with this picture?

The handsome man was sitting miles away on the other side of the couch. The handsome man was not interested. Or maybe he was, but wasn't going to do anything about it, which resulted in the same thing.

Now, granted, after an uncontrollable boo-hooing

session, she probably had a blotchy face, swollen eyes and a red nose, and she hoped that waterproof mascara was also tearproof. But candlelight wasn't all that bright, was it?

How could he be completely unaffected by their circumstances? No doubt he thought he was being noble by not taking advantage of the situation.

Did she have to fall for the last noble man in the universe?

Her eyes stung. Great. She still had tears left.

She sipped her champagne and hoped Justin couldn't tell she was getting weepy again. He'd been wonderful to her, even though she'd rather have been alone, since he was the reason she was crying.

Instead of acknowledging that they had the beginning of something special, he announced with depressing regularity his intention to date the entire female population of Memphis.

Her mother and sisters would know what to do in this situation. They knew how to hook a man, but good. Only, Hayley couldn't ask them how because they thought she'd already hooked this one.

They'd congratulated her, and they were happy for her. But though they'd never say so to her face, Hayley knew they couldn't figure out how she'd attracted a man like Justin—Sloane. And of course, she hadn't.

She gazed around the room again. With all this material to work with, even Medusa would have inspired a pass by now. Talk about depressing. She sniffed. This was absolutely the worst Valentine's Day in her entire life.

HAYLEY WAS STILL UNHAPPY. She was trying to hide it, but every so often, the candlelight caught a glint in her eye, and she'd just sniffed for the first time in a while.

"Do you want to talk about it?" Justin asked, half hoping she would and half hoping she wouldn't.

She gave him a look he couldn't read, then started talking. "Some little girls spend a lot of time imagining their weddings. I never did, so I thought I was immune to the allure of the fantasy wedding—especially after enduring my sisters' productions. And yet today, I realized I wasn't immune at all. Today was probably the only wedding I'll ever have and...and it wasn't even *my* wedding."

Justin remembered thinking that this was more her mother's farewell to Memphis than her daughter's wedding. "Hayley, you'll find somebody," he forced himself to say, not all that taken with the idea.

Get over it unless you're prepared to claim her for yourself.

"Yeah, sure." She sniffed again. "And then I get to say, 'Oh, by the way, this is my first marriage, but my second wedding. Just ignore all those comments about my ex-husband.'"

Justin knew laughter was *not* the correct response here. "If you explain the circumstances, he'll understand."

"Maybe."

"If he loves you, he will."

She gave him a sad smile. "And you don't think he'll be appalled at what I've done? Even I'm appalled at how everything snowballed until all I could do was roll along with it."

Justin knew exactly what she meant. "I was snowballing right along with you."

She twisted the clump of tissues in her hand. "I think what I really hate about all this is that when I announce my divorce, all those people are going to think it's because I couldn't hang on to you. They can't imagine how I managed to attract you in the first place."

"That's not true." But Justin realized he was trying to convince himself more than Hayley. He wished she hadn't noticed all the comments. "And...the guy you marry should not only understand what you did, he should admire you for it. You let your mother have her dream at the expense of your own." He reached out and tucked her hair behind her ear. Yes, she was crying again.

Obviously, her self-confidence had taken a beating. "Hayley." He leaned closer because she'd turned her head away. "You're smart and fun to be with, and you can find humor in absurd situations. Any man would be lucky to—"

"If I'm such a prize, then why aren't you attracted to me?" She glared at him through tears.

Didn't she know? Couldn't she tell? "I am. But I'm not in a position to act on that attraction."

"Your passion overwhelms me." She took their empty plates and walked over to set them on the table. On the way, she passed by the candles.

Justin saw her in slow motion...saw her legs...saw the outline of her torso.... And she thought he wasn't attracted to her? What about those kisses they'd exchanged? He thought they were pretty potent—at least for him they were. Maybe she was used to potent kisses. Maybe they weren't anything special to her.

The thought didn't sit well with him.

Hayley floated back to the couch, gave him a you're-an-insect look and dabbed at her eyes.

That did it. "My passion might not overwhelm you, but it's about to overwhelm me." Justin was angry and getting angrier. "I've listened to you whine and cry, and now it's your turn to listen to me. I've been upfront with you from the beginning about not being in a position to start any kind of relationship. I've still got debts to pay off, first and foremost the one to Ross. I *will* pay it back as fast as possible. In the meantime, I'm not going to take advantage of you or any artificially romantic situations." Her eyes widened, but Justin's frustration had been building.

"Yes, your sisters are very beautiful, and they make it clear that they expect men to tell them so. And you know what?"

She shook her head.

"It's annoying. I never felt that way with you until right now. But if you want me to tell you that you're beautiful and that I can hardly keep my hands off you, then I will!"

"You think I'm beautiful?" she asked in a small voice.

That's all she'd heard? He nodded and watched her smile. Swallowing, he added, "And the hands part—don't forget that. It's important."

"I do think hands are very important." Somehow she'd drifted right next to him. She lifted his hand and placed it palm to palm with hers.

"Hayley," he said sternly. At least he was trying for stern. There was a little too much question at the end.

Hayley took her index finger and traced the outline of his hand, and he discovered how sensitive the nerve endings in the webbing of his fingers could be.

"Don't worry. You've been crystal clear. No strings. No promises."

His hand was on fire. "We shouldn't."

Up and down. Up and down. "Shouldn't what? We haven't done anything."

Not yet. He shuddered.

"Are you cold? I'm hot." Languidly she fanned herself, first with her hand, then with the flimsy edge of her robe.

It caught the edge of his champagne, sending half a flute full of liquid down the front of her robe.

Her gasp broke the trance he seemed to have fallen into. "Sorry," he said, and grabbed for a cloth napkin.

"It's not your fault." Hayley stood and removed her robe, using the napkin to dab at the nightgown underneath.

And that's when Justin discovered the amazingly transparent qualities of wet chiffon. The wine had splashed over her left breast and dripped in streams down the side. Between that and the candles silhouetting the rest of her, he decided she was the most beautiful, desirable, tempting woman in the world.

But he'd already known that, hadn't he?

Hayley pulled the wet fabric away from her body and blew, like that was going to do anything.

All she accomplished was to blow away the last tiny particle of rational thought Justin had left. That could only explain his next thought which was, if he'd shown restraint and she'd looked at him with contempt, then how would she look at him if he showed no restraint at all?

His ears buzzed, a sure sign that his thinking was wrong.

So he stopped thinking.

He stood and silently approached her. Stopping directly in front of her, he held out his hand.

"Oh, I've got it," she said, bending over to dab her thigh where champagne had rolled before soaking in.

"Let me."

Something in his voice made her look questioningly at him. She dropped the damp napkin into his palm. "I should rinse this out...."

Starting at her throat, his eyes never leaving hers, Justin slowly trailed the napkin over her breast, her stomach and thigh. The wet fabric stuck to her skin. He dropped the napkin to the floor.

Her eyes were wide, staring into his.

Deliberately, Justin allowed his gaze to drift over the same path he'd drawn the napkin then float back to her eyes.

Her breathing increased. She glanced down, then gasped as she saw herself. "Oh, I should—" She broke off as he captured the hand she'd moved to cover her breast. Her lips parted.

He lowered his head and she raised hers. She probably thought he was going to kiss her. And he was.

But not on her mouth.

He'd shown restraint and she'd been hurt. He'd played by the rules and she'd been scornful.

Life is short. Eat dessert first. Maybe it was time to follow Ross's advice.

Justin started at the top edge of the spill, just above the swell of her breast. He both heard and felt her gasp as his lips touched her. His tongue tasted the champagne, chiffon and skin. He lightly sucked until the champagne flavor was gone, then moved lower.

"What are you doing?" she whispered as she inhaled.

"Eating dessert first," he whispered back, liking how his breath made her tremble.

Or was he trembling?

Justin worked his way lower. Hayley clutched his shoulders and threw her head back.

He was almost to the tip of her breast. He could hear his pulse pounding in his ears. He could feel each minute thread of the chiffon with his tongue.

"Justin!"

Justin's mouth closed over her, sucking out every bit of champagne and some of the chiffon flavoring, too. His hands roamed over her body. The chiffon was like nothing. And soon there was nothing, nothing but a pool of chiffon with Hayley standing in the middle.

The starlight, the candlelight, whichever it was that made her look like a dream woman, Justin didn't know. She was beyond beautiful and he tried to tell her so, but wasn't certain if he managed to speak the words.

It didn't seem to matter. Hayley was in his arms, kissing him and murmuring his name.

Justin was happy—giddily happy. Happy in an immature, juvenile way that he'd never felt before.

He helped her take off his shirt, nearly passing out from the pleasure of experiencing her skin next to his. Soft womanly skin, covering curves and hollows he longed to explore.

Soft womanly fingers unbelted his trousers and soon he was standing in a pant pool. It did not have the same romantic effect as Hayley's chiffon pool, and they both laughed.

Shared laughter. This wasn't the first time Hayley had understood without words. It was one of the things he lo—liked best about her.

She looked him frankly up and down. "My sisters are right. You *are* worth waiting for." Wrapping her arms around him, she whispered, "Don't get off the boat in Vicksburg." She kissed his throat.

How could he leave the boat—and Hayley—in Vicksburg?

He kissed her hard and fast, then held her tightly, afraid to let her go.

And that was when he knew he must.

If he made love to her now, he wouldn't be *able* to let her go.

Lacing their hands together, Hayley stepped back, pulling him toward the bed.

Justin didn't move. "I can't."

Her other hand encircled him. "Oh, yes you can."

The blood rushed in his ears with such force, Justin was certain his eardrums would burst.

And he wouldn't feel a thing, since all sensory awareness and any conscious thought had relocated to his groin.

Before moving toward the bed again, Hayley picked the champagne bottle out of the ice bucket. "If we're lucky, I might spill this, too." She held it up and several drops of icy water landed on Justin.

They were tiny drops, but they were enough to restore brain function.

"Hayley—no." Regretfully, and she'd never know how regretfully, he shook his head.

"No? Why not?"

He took the bottle and replaced it in the ice bucket. "Sex with you would mean too much."

"And this is a bad thing?"

"Right now, yes."

"Why?"

"Hayley, my parents got married when they were still in high school because my mother was pregnant with me."

"If you're worried about *that*, then you haven't seen the prize basket I won from Martin's Drug Emporium." She pointed to a white basket with a huge red bow on the floor beside the canopy bed.

An unwilling chuckle escaped him. "It's not just *that*," he mimicked her, then sobered. "You want more from me than I can give you."

Slowly she reached behind him for the champagne,

allowing her body to touch his. "From where I stand, it looks like you can give me quite a lot."

He couldn't think when she was touching him. He didn't *want* to think when she was touching him.

He wanted to touch her back. And why shouldn't he? Justin had been denying himself for years, sticking with his goals, never wavering, waiting to collect his reward: happiness.

Being with Hayley made him happy. If he made love to her, he'd be ecstatic. And if his ultimate goal was happiness and it was right within his grasp, or rather was currently grasping him, then why wait?

Hayley stuck her finger in the end of the champagne bottle and tilted it. When she withdrew her finger, bubbles clung to it.

She drew her finger across his lips.

The reason why he shouldn't make love to her fizzed away along with the bubbles.

Hayley tilted the bottle until champagne dribbled onto her breasts. "Oops," she said.

The drops of champagne glistened in the candlelight.

Kneeling, Justin caught a drop with his tongue and followed it all the way up to the source, switched to another trail and traveled back down again.

Hayley's breath came in short gasps and she clutched at his shoulders. She moaned his name.

There were too many champagne trails for him to remain standing here. Feeling a kinship with ancient cavemen, Justin knocked her knees out from under her and swooped her up as she fell.

"Justin!" she squealed.

He carried her to the bed.

"Justin." She sighed when he set her gently down.

He took the champagne bottle from her and poured some new trails, making it a personal rule to keep his tongue strictly on the paths forged by the champagne.

Hayley wiggled and squirmed. "Justin," she pleaded.

"Rules are rules," he murmured, bypassing the peaks for the valleys.

"Juuustinnnn," she begged.

She'd made his name into a complete vocabulary.

He decided to reward her by veering off the trails.

Hayley responded by pulling him on top of her. "It's time to break open the gift basket."

He raised himself onto his elbows and stared down at her. "Now? As in right now?"

Hayley nipped his earlobe. "Yes."

When he'd thought of making love with her, he'd imagined hours of exploring each other. "Are you sure? We can take this slow."

In answer, she reached for the gift basket. "We will. Later."

But after they had to use their teeth to tear the shrinkwrap, Justin figured the moment was gone.

Fine with him, he thought as he took her lips in a long, slow, lingering kiss that produced the tiny moan in the back of her throat that he loved so much. He wanted Hayley to experience passion as no one had ever experienced passion before. He wanted her thrashing. He wanted her moaning. He wanted her on the edge. He wanted her eyes glazed. He wanted her panting. He wanted—

"Justin!" Hayley grabbed him and rocked forward.

Justin inhaled sharply. "Hayley, you can't do that to a man and expect him to wait!"

"Don't wait. I'm not," she said, and exploded around him with a force that left them both gasping.

Justin was on the edge. "Incredible," he breathed as he moved. Seconds later, his shudders echoed hers.

It was passion as he'd never experienced it before. He gulped air as though he'd run a marathon. He blinked, certain his eyes were glazed. He'd thrash, but he didn't want to move.

It wasn't possible to feel better than this.

Hayley purred. That was the only way to describe the satisfied sound she made when she wrapped her legs around him.

Justin wanted her never to let go. Never ever.

Gradually their breathing slowed.

Gradually Justin began to think again.

Hayley stretched, squeezing him in the process. "I am *ravenously* hungry." She smiled up at him.

Justin had thought she was beautiful before. Now she was radiant. Glowing.

And he realized she was in love with him. The committed kind of love. The let's-get-married kind of love.

The too-soon kind of love.

The knowledge filled him with dread. What had he done?

"Let's get something to eat," she suggested, sliding her legs down his. "We've got the rest of tonight and six more gloriously, stupendously wonderful days ahead of us."

Justin managed a smile. Hayley didn't seem to notice his silence. Unselfconsciously she rose from the bed, talking all the while about the rest of the trip to New Orleans and the stops along the way.

She was making plans, plans that included him. Plans that assumed they'd be together in spite of what he'd told her.

He'd known making love to her would change everything. He'd tried to explain....

It was all happening too fast. Getting to know her, his growing feelings, the sex—everything was too fast. Justin needed time to absorb all the changes and the impact they had on his life. He needed time to figure out what he was going to do. He couldn't toss away a lifetime goal based on a few minutes of mind-numbing pleasure. Above all, he couldn't put either Hayley or himself through the struggles his parents had gone through.

With an excited exclamation, she pulled him toward the window. Naked, they stood and looked out onto the lights of Vicksburg, Mississippi.

Oblivious to his inner turmoil, Hayley chatted happily as she scarfed down the hors d'oeuvres. "After the six days here, what about the Puerto Rican cruise? I wasn't going on it, but we can if you like. Can you get more vacation?"

More vacation? With the computer situation at his office, he couldn't even get *this* vacation. He and Sloane apparently had something in common after all. "No."

"Oh, come on." She pressed her body against his and traced her finger along his jaw. "It'll be fun. We'll make love for days and days—"

"No!" Didn't she remember what he'd told her? Didn't she understand? Justin stepped away from her. "In fact, I...I should leave now." Or he never would.

"*What?*"

Justin's hands were cold, so he didn't touch her. It was probably for the best. "I need time."

"Time for what?"

"To—to think."

"To think about *what?*"

Justin gestured all around them. "Hayley, I'm not ready for all this."

Hayley stood there, looking at him, incredulity in her eyes. "So you're just going to leave?"

He nodded.

"Even after we..." Her gaze darted to the bed, then around the room, and Justin realized she was searching for something to cover herself. After taking a step toward the discarded chiffon pool, she went to the closet, running her hands over the gowns hanging there. Justin heard her make a small frustrated sound before grabbing the bright, orange flowered short kimono and tying it in a tight bow.

Then she looked at him.

And then she looked away.

This is what happened when a man followed one set of instincts when he should be following another. Mumbling something—he wasn't sure what—Justin drew on his pants.

"I'd like to hear an explanation," she announced as Justin pulled on his shirt.

"Not that there could be any acceptable explanation," she continued. "I just want to hear one so I can tell you how stupid it is."

"I don't consider what happened to my parents to be 'stupid.' Mom dropped out of high school and never graduated. They struggled along until my dad left us when I was four. The whole time he resented me for 'stealing his fun,' as he put it. Felt he'd missed a big part of life. I remember the arguments and I remember my mother crying. They weren't ready for marriage and children."

"Justin, they were, what...seventeen? Eighteen? No education? You're almost thirty! You're a lawyer. We have condoms. There is no comparison."

"But there is! I worked from the time I could push a lawn mower. There has never been a period in my life when I've not been struggling for money, or when I could kick back and have fun. I missed out on all the after-school clubs and sports, hanging around the malls on weekends—all of that, because I was always working. It was the same in college. I was either working or studying. Nothing else. Teaching high school showed me how much I'd missed—and even then, I was going to law school at night. I'm not going to make the same mistake my parents did. I'm not going to commit to a relationship before I've had a chance to experience the stuff I missed as a kid."

She'd listened to him with a face of stone. "So, you're still worried about what you might miss...say, hanging out at a mall—and who you might miss it with—if you stay with me?"

Put that way, it made him sound like a jerk. Maybe it would be easier if she thought he was a jerk. And maybe he was. "How long do you think we'd have together before I resented you the way my father resented my mother and me?" he asked at last.

"That won't happen."

Echoing through Justin's memory were the shouts of his immature father and the crying pleadings of his helpless mother. "I'm not willing to take that chance."

Hayley looked at him for a long moment, her arms crossed over her chest. "In that case, I guess you'd better leave."

9

HAYLEY STAYED on the *Mississippi Princess* all the way to New Orleans. At each stop, she half expected to see Justin dash on board to tell her that he was an idiot and had made a huge mistake.

He *was* an idiot and he *had* made a huge mistake. She completely understood the reasoning behind his reluctance to commit to a relationship—if a six-day cruise counted as a relationship—before he was ready. She just didn't agree with it. They weren't two undereducated teenagers with a baby. A relationship, or, yes, even marriage, didn't have to be the prison his parents had made it.

Unfortunately, Justin wouldn't be convinced until he'd seen and experienced the malls of the world. He was determined to have fun whether it made him miserable or not.

The trapped expression in his eyes that night had convinced Hayley that arguing was pointless.

Well, she wasn't going to beg and she wasn't going to hang around and wait, either. However, should she get the chance, she intended to make Justin see the error of his ways. He'd have to call her first, though. She only hoped she could hold out before doing something stupid, like calling him instead.

Reaching New Orleans, Hayley refused the Puerto Rican cruise, thinking her tax bill was high enough already, and flew home to Memphis, where she hid out in her apartment and lived on the frozen dinners, chocolate and videos she'd stockpiled in advance.

She ran out after three days.

"Of course you ran out," she mumbled as she searched through her freezer. "You weren't supposed to eat spaghetti carbonera for breakfast. At least not two at a time."

If she stuffed her hair under a baseball cap, wore sunglasses and drove to a different neighborhood, she could risk a trip to the grocery store.

Driving by her mother's house on the way back from the store wasn't smart. Hayley hadn't meant to turn down the street, but when she saw the moving van, how could she not? She'd known her mother was vacating the house by the end of February, but hadn't realized how close the end of February was.

Drat these short months anyway.

She parked as close as she dared, then watched as pieces of her childhood were carried into the van.

Her mother was happy, or at least she'd seemed so when Hayley had called her after landing in New Orleans. Basking in the afterglow of Hayley's triumphant wedding, she gushed on about the duplex she was buying in Sun City.

Hayley did not tell her Sloane had returned to El Bahar.

Hayley did not tell her Justin had returned to Memphis.

Hayley did not tell her she'd never been more miserable in her life. She was happy for her mother. She was miserable for herself.

"I'M NOT GOING to charge Hayley for my services as best man," Ross said from the hammock in his living room. "I won enough money gambling."

"Good," Justin replied. He would have made Ross give Hayley back the money anyway. He poured a white liquid out of the blender. "Are you sure you should be drinking piña coladas?"

"I'm not taking any medication and I'm not drinking. I'm sipping for atmosphere and research." Ross held out his hand for the glass.

Justin handed it to him and turned down the fan. "It's freezing in here!"

"Ocean breezes can be quite nippy." Ross looked at the drink. "No pineapple spears?"

"I don't think World War II sailors put pineapple spears in their drinks. In fact, I doubt they diluted their rum at all." Since Ross had stacked his chairs on top of the sofa to make room for the hammock, Justin sat on the floor.

"Then how did they drink it?"

"Out of the bottle," Justin said.

Ross grimaced. Setting the drink down on the carpet, he put opaque plastic sunglasses over his eyes. "Turn on the sunlamp, okay?"

"You'll fry your skin."

"I only want a little color. The sailors have been on Bali Hai. They'll have color."

"Won't the play people have stage makeup?"

Ross grimaced. "Theater company, please." He lifted his glasses and looked at Justin. "My character needs this, Justin."

Justin switched on the lamp.

"Your character needs to call Hayley," Ross continued, replacing his glasses.

"Can't you manage to go more than ten minutes without mentioning Hayley?"

"No. I like her. She likes you."

Justin had been tormented by this liking. Ross had no idea of what had transpired between Justin and Hayley in the bridal suite of the *Mississippi Princess* and Justin wasn't going to tell him. The time spent making love with Hayley had been the best and the worst of his life.

In the two weeks since Justin had walked off the *Mississippi Princess* in Vicksburg, there hadn't been a minute when he wasn't thinking of Hayley. Even though the corrupted data at the IRS had resulted in mountains of returns to be reexamined, so that every moment of his workday was filled to capacity, he thought of her and wondered what she was doing. Wondered if she was thinking of him.

He had to get her out of his mind. She was interfering with his work, interfering with his sleep. Interfering with his friendship with Ross, who alternated between telling him he was an idiot and exhorting him to call her.

Justin needed time to think, but how could he get time to think when she occupied his thoughts?

"The phone is right over there," Ross said, pointing blindly.

"Suppose I did call her.... What would I say to her?" Justin asked.

"How about, 'Please go out with me because I'm utterly wretched and making Ross's life wretched, too'?"

"I can't."

"Why not?"

"Because I'd never recover from having a relationship with her and ruining it."

"*Hello?* That's what you've done, buddy."

Justin's jaw grew tight. "It's better this way."

"What way?" Sitting up, Ross took off his sunglasses. "Look at you. You aren't sleeping. I can't find anything good to eat in your refrigerator, and you're giving the IRS tons of free overtime. It's all because of your cockamamie plan, isn't it?"

In spite of his heartache, Justin smiled.

"All right, then, get on with your plan already. If you won't call Hayley, then call someone else."

"I don't want to call anyone else."

"Then call Hayley. She won't wait forever, you know."

"I don't want her waiting. She needs to find someone else."

Ross blinked at him. "So you think you can get over her if she's not available?"

"Well...yeah."

Ross blinked again. "Okay, then let's find her somebody else."

"What do you mean?"

Ross put on his sunglasses and repositioned himself under the lamp. "Let's hurry the process along so you can get on with your pursuit of frivolity and meaningless relationships."

Justin didn't like the way that sounded, but there was no talking with Ross when he was in one of his moods.

"If I recall, your office is teeming with unmarried men."

"Not *teeming*—"

"Who interrupted our lunch that time...you know the overeager assistant of yours?"

"Larry? No way. Hayley wouldn't—"

"Here's the plan—you like plans, don't you, Justin?"

Justin glared at Ross.

"You call Hayley about her taxes—you've been worried about her taxes, haven't you?"

"Yes, but—"

"So call her and ask her to come to your office. Throw Larry at her and see what happens."

"Nothing will happen."

"You sure?"

No, Justin wasn't sure. He didn't like feeling unsure. "It's a stupid plan."

"And you know all about stupid plans, don't you?"

Justin drew a deep breath. "Ross—"

"Call her. Right now, while I'm here to badger you."

Justin chuckled. It was hard to stay angry with Ross, and he meant well.

Justin might as well call her. Hayley would probably

slam the phone in his ear, and then Ross would drop the subject.

"The phone's on the bar. I've conveniently posted her number by it. Use the taxes excuse."

THE PHONE INTERRUPTED Hayley's glorious orgy of junk food. "Hello?" she managed to answer while munching on caramel popcorn.

"Hayley?"

She swallowed, or tried to. Unchewed caramel popcorn didn't swallow well. "Justin?"

"Yes... How did it go?"

How did what go? Waking up without him? The cruise? Hiding from the world? Watching her mother leave the house Hayley'd grown up in, and not being there to help? Getting over him? "Fine."

"Good."

Awkward silence reigned. Hayley was not, not, *not* going to ask why he'd called. "How's Ross?"

"Fine."

"Good."

More silence. It was his turn. She'd wait.

"Uh, do you remember me telling you that I'd like to see your papers with the valuations for the wedding prizes?"

"No."

"I did."

"I don't remember."

"Sure, I did. It was when... Maybe I didn't say it out loud, but I thought, if you'd like me to, I could take a look at them and see if the values are inflated. You could challenge and reduce your tax bill."

How romantic. Almost as romantic as being rejected in favor of hanging out at a mall. Did he really think he could call her and talk taxes like nothing had happened between them? Did he really think she wanted anything to do with him? Did he really think she'd agree to see him again?

She opened her mouth to tell him exactly what she thought of him. "Okay." *Hayley, you are so weak.*

"Great. Let me know when it's convenient, and we'll set up an appointment."

Hayley pulled the phone away from her ear and stared at it. She couldn't believe this man had seen her naked. "I have to go back to work tomorrow. I can't take any more time off, so if you want to see me during work hours, it'll have to be on my lunch hour."

"Is Monday okay?"

Monday? *Monday?* When an entire weekend loomed ahead of them? "Monday is just hunky-dory." She punched the disconnect button, thinking that it wasn't nearly as satisfying as slamming down the phone.

JUSTIN HAD a vague feeling that all had not gone well during his conversation with Hayley, but he wasn't sure until Monday noon rolled around and she walked into his office at the IRS building.

Then he knew.

The first clue he had was the way she was dressed. She wore a suit in a pale color and what he first assumed was a white blouse underneath. Ignoring the deliberate positioning of the chairs in front of his desk, Hayley snagged one and drew it around to his side, sat down and crossed her legs.

"How was Puerto Rico?" he asked.

"I didn't go. I decided I couldn't afford to."

Then she'd been back for a week already. He could have seen her days ago. He could have...

Her suit jacket fell open and a glitter caught his eye. The last time he'd seen that beading, it was on her wedding gown and the corset...the corset beneath it. The same corset she was now wearing so the entire world could see it.

Or maybe she was deliberately tormenting him.

And he was definitely tormented.

"Been hanging around any malls lately?" she asked, swinging her leg ever so slightly.

That was his second clue that Hayley was blisteringly angry with him.

There were more clues after that, but he stopped counting.

Gesturing toward the brown envelope she held, he asked, "Shall I take a look at those receipts?"

"Sure." Hayley leaned over unnecessarily far when handing him the packet.

Justin's mouth went dry.

"Do you mind if I kick off my shoe?" she asked. "These are new and are giving me a blister."

"Go ahead."

She flashed him a bright cheery smile, then bent down and massaged her foot. "That feels *so* much better." She closed her eyes, her head tilted back. "Mmm," she murmured deep in her throat.

It reminded Justin of the little moan... It *was* the little moan.

"Oh, yeeesss," she breathed, still rubbing her foot.

Sweat collected under his shirt collar. His palms dampened. After fumbling with the clasp on the envelope, he withdrew the papers and tried to study them.

"Hmm."

Don't look. Don't listen. Blindly he grabbed one. "What was this for?"

Hayley released her foot and opened her eyes, which was what he'd been hoping she'd do. But then she stood and leaned next to him, which *wasn't* what he'd been hoping she'd do—at least the part of his body he vowed to think with hadn't been hoping in that direction. The other part of his body was sending him urgent messages, alerting him to her close proximity.

"That's the prize from the lingerie shop." She pointed to the clearly labeled form. "I used it all and then some. The white peignoir alone cost... You remember the white peignoir, don't you?"

Her hair brushed his cheek as she turned her head to gaze into his eyes.

Of course he remembered the white peignoir. She was baiting him.

"It was worth every penny," he said. She was so close, her features blurred out of focus, but Justin wasn't going to move forward, and kiss her, nor backward, and let her know he was uncomfortable.

Slowly Hayley straightened and returned to her

chair. She remained blessedly silent as Justin studied the receipts. "Did you receive the cash difference between the portion of the gift certificates you spent and the face value of the certificates themselves?"

Hayley shook her head.

"That might be worth investigating." As he'd planned with Ross, Justin paged Larry Thorston, the paralegal assigned to their department.

Half a minute later, Larry appeared in the doorway. "You rang, Master?"

Larry was two or three years younger than Justin. Hayley's age, maybe. He was blond, dressed well and was thinking of going to law school himself.

And he was giving Hayley the once-over.

"Larry, I need these reference binders." Justin handed a paper to him. "And when you bring them, would you do me a favor and take Hayley for coffee—or maybe lunch? I don't want her getting bored while I read up on prizes."

Hayley and the paralegal spoke at the same time.

"I'm not bored," Hayley said.

"Sure thing!" Larry looked dazed with his good fortune and sprinted down the hall.

"I'll be reading some very dry case rulings," Justin told Hayley. "I don't want you to miss lunch. Larry's a great guy. Lots of stories. Ask him about his boat. He'll keep you entertained." Bored, most likely, Justin thought with inappropriate satisfaction.

Hayley narrowed her eyes, and then Larry came back with the binders. He grinned, resembling a great big, drooling golden retriever.

Hayley gave Justin a look, then smiled at Larry as she stood and stepped into her shoes. It was her big, wide Hayley smile. The smile Justin thought was his. She was smiling *his* smile at dumb old Larry, who looked like he'd been smacked in the head.

"Thank you, Larry," she said, and looped her arm through his. "See you later, Justin." She waggled her fingers, then smiled again at Larry.

Justin held himself rigidly upright until they'd passed out of sight. Then he slowly lowered his head to his desk and moaned.

Why did doing the right thing feel so wrong?

HAYLEY WENT OUT with Larry. But he wasn't Justin, so she didn't go out with him again.

Then Ross called her to invite her to the opening of *South Pacific*. She was seated between another lawyer from Justin's office, and Sean, an actor friend of Ross's.

Justin was two rows behind her, so Hayley flirted with both men. And both men asked her out. She would have declined, except she thought Justin might have overheard and been jealous.

But apparently he wasn't. At least he didn't act like it at the cast party afterward when he didn't even approach her.

"Hayley, dear, I'm worried about you," Ross said when he called her a week later. "Sean said you barely spoke two words when he took you out."

Hayley felt guilty. She shouldn't have gone out with Sean. He was a perfectly nice man, but he wasn't Justin. "I'm sorry."

"You need to perk up," Ross advised her. "You don't want Justin to think you're moping around because of him, do you?"

"I don't care what Justin thinks."

"Of course you do. You want him to realize that he's been an idiot. You want him to admit that he made the biggest mistake of his life when he let you go."

Uncanny. "How did you know?" Hayley asked in a small voice.

"I have a gift. Now listen. Justin and I ran into a friend of his, a Bryant Williams. He coaches something at the high school where Justin used to teach. He's divorced, no kids, and is just getting back into the dating scene. I told him about you."

"Oh, Ross, I don't think—"

"And Justin *glared*."

Hayley stopped protesting. "He did?"

"Definitely. So I want you to go out with Bryant and be friendly and upbeat. We want him raving about you."

"Ross, I appreciate what you're trying to do, but it wouldn't be fair to Bryant."

"Why not? You may fall madly in love with him."

Fat chance, Hayley wanted to say, but Ross had a point. Justin wasn't the only man in the world. "Okay," she agreed. "I'll go out with Bryant."

"Great," Ross said. "Now, let's discuss wardrobe."

HAYLEY STARED at herself in the dressing room mirror. What had she been thinking, to go shopping with Ross, of all people? She should have known better than to accept fashion advice from a man who'd been hit on the head.

There was no way she was going to appear in public, let alone buy, the black leather miniskirt, bustier and cropped jacket he'd insisted she try on.

She looked like a male fantasy cartoon character, especially now that she'd put on the boots. She could hear her mother and sisters screaming, "Trashy!" then telling her to remove the bustier and wear flat shoes and she'd look just precious.

Pushing open the white slatted door, Hayley stepped out of the dressing room. "Ross, this isn't—"

Standing next to Ross's chair was a dark-haired man wearing a suit and a harried expression. Justin. "You promised you'd buy new tires," he was saying. "I can't believe you bought a hammock and a sunlamp instead of tires. I'm not going to keep rescuing you." He glanced up at Hayley and froze.

Ross stepped into the breach. "Hayley!" He leapt out of his chair. "You look marvelous. Doesn't she look marvelous, Justin?"

Justin didn't answer, but his gaze roamed over her.

Hayley felt hot and tingly. She thought leather was supposed to breathe.

"I think this outfit will make a good impression on Bryant," Ross said. "What's your opinion, Justin? You know him better than I do."

"You're going out with Bryant Williams?" Justin asked her.

Hayley tossed her hair over her shoulder. "Yes."

He gestured to the leather outfit. "And you're planning to wear *that?*"

Not until that instant. What business was it of Justin's *what* she wore? "Think he'll like it?" She pirouetted.

Justin's look of disgust was directed toward Ross.

"Well." Ross clapped his hands together. "Hayley, I do appreciate your offer of a ride, but since Justin was able to make it after all, I'll leave with him."

Justin still stared at her, his gaze a dark blue.

"Justin?" Ross tugged on his sleeve.

Hayley knew Ross had set up this situation, but she didn't mind. Not after seeing Justin's stunned expression.

She decided to buy the outfit. It sent the perfect message: You made a *big* mistake.

BRYANT WILLIAMS WAS a huge Elvis fan. They were meeting at Graceland, then going out for barbecue. This alone told Hayley that they had nothing in common, but she decided to keep the date, anyway. And she kept it while wearing the leather outfit.

She parked her car and made her way to the Graceland ticket office. Standing by the booth was a large, burly man, who could only be an ex-football player.

"Are you Bryant?" she asked, approaching him, her feet already protesting the high-heeled boots. He looked moderately handsome. Not in Justin's league, but okay.

He blinked. "Ma'am?"

"I'm Hayley Parrish."

"Pleased to meet you."

When he continued to stand there, she asked, "Are you Bryant?"

"Yes, oh, yes, ma'am."

Hayley smiled. "I'm your date."

"You're my date?" A big goofy grin stole across his face. "Next time you see ole Ross, tell him I owe him one."

Okay. It appeared that men of all kinds had a thing for black leather. Nice to know, but she didn't need to know it now.

He turned to face the ticket office. "I do believe, ma'am—"

"Hayley."

"I do believe, Hayley, ma'am, that I'll spring for the Platinum Tour Package."

"What's that?" she asked as they stood in line.

"That gets us into everything here."

"You know, you don't have to do that. I like Elvis Presley's music, but I'm not a platinum sort of fan."

"You will be when I finish showing you Graceland."

Hayley sighed inwardly. Her feet weren't platinum fans, either, especially in these boots.

Bryant spurned the headphones, conducting his own commentary of the Graceland Mansion with its jungle den and TV room. He explained the significance of every exhibit in the trophy building, and then, cautioning her to silence, though she hadn't been very vocal up until now, led her to the Meditation Garden, where Elvis was buried.

A familiar figure contemplated the headstone.

"Ross?" Hayley approached him.

She was shushed on all sides.

"Hello, Bryant, Hayley," he whispered. "Nice outfit."

"Ross, what are you doing here?" she asked suspiciously, wondering if Justin was also here.

"Please show some respect," whispered a teary-eyed woman.

"I am, madam," Ross announced. "I am absorbing the essence of Elvis Presley so that I can adequately portray the King."

"You're going to be an Elvis impersonator?" From the horrified looks on the faces of Bryant and those around her, Hayley knew immediately that it was the wrong thing to say.

"I am going to be singing a musical tribute to the King nightly on the *Mississippi Princess*," Ross corrected, and redeemed himself in the eyes of those present.

Hayley obviously was beyond redemption, probably because of the leather. "Congratulations," she whispered to Ross.

After another round of shushing, she decided to wait for Bryant outside.

Some minutes later, Bryant rejoined her, wiping his eyes. "Would you like to see the Automobile Museum now?"

Actually, Hayley was ready to sit down, but she smiled and after another hour, was finally seated across from Bryant in the Chrome Grille, a restaurant near the museum.

They'd ordered barbecue and were waiting for their food, when Ross and Justin entered the restaurant.

JUSTIN SAW HAYLEY at once. She was wearing the leather outfit and she was smiling at Bryant. He was smiling back.

And why wouldn't he be? He was with the hottest-looking woman in the room.

Just then, Hayley leaned forward and propped her chin on her hand.

Justin's mouth went dry and he wanted to tell her to sit up straight.

Justin had always thought Bryant was a great guy. But he was a great *divorced* guy. And he hadn't dated anybody seriously since the divorce. That meant he was hungry, and there was Hayley, serving herself up on a platter.

"Why, look. It's Hayley and Bryant." Ross waved, using exaggerated movements that drew the stares of everyone in the place.

"You are in big trouble," Justin murmured.

"I am *offended* by your implication."

"I'm not implying anything. I'm saying outright that you knew they were going to be here when you called asking me to meet you."

Ross gave him an amused look and headed for their table.

"Ross!" Justin hissed, but Ross ignored him.

Justin could either remain where he was and look foolish, or follow Ross and possibly head off disaster.

He followed.

"Hayley! Bryant!" boomed Ross.

"Still here, Ross?" Hayley asked, glancing at Justin, then away.

Still here? Justin scowled at Ross.

"Yes, I continue to absorb. I feel I can bring an added, though unworthy, dimension to the King's songs now." Ross beamed at them, giving no indication that he intended to find another table.

"Well, good seeing you," Justin said, hinting that they should move on.

Ross ignored the hint. "It's serendipity, that's what it is."

"Why don't you join us?" Bryant spoke as though the words were dragged out of him.

"What a *splendid* idea," Ross said with Shakespearean exaggeration, and promptly seated himself.

Hayley looked trapped.

Justin knew how she felt.

Bryant was making a valiant effort to appear pleased, but he wasn't quite the actor Ross was.

"Ross." Justin tried one last time. "Let's not intrude."

"We're not intruding!" Ross proclaimed in a way that allowed no disagreement. "Stop fussing and sit down."

Justin knew when he was beaten. But *fussing?* Ross was going to pay dearly later.

A waitress brought Hayley and Bryant's food—great plates of barbecue ribs that hung over the edge.

"We'll have the same thing," Ross told the waitress. "Please. Go ahead and eat," he directed.

With visible relief, Bryant did so.

Hayley stared at her plate.

"Don't be shy," Ross said. "Just tuck that napkin right... Well, there doesn't seem to be any place to tuck it, does there?"

"Ross!" Justin frowned at him.

Ross looked innocently baffled, but Justin knew what he was doing—he was drawing attention to Hayley, that's what he was doing.

Hayley tossed her head back and laughed. "That's all right, Justin. In fact it's so warm in here, I think I'll take off my jacket."

Ross gave her an approving smile.

Justin gripped the edge of the table.

Ross, who clearly had an agenda, helped Hayley off with her jacket.

Hayley's creamy skin—and lots of it—contrasted with the leather in a way that made Justin's teeth ache.

He glared furiously at Ross.

Ross met Justin's gaze with his sweetly sad, wise smile, his noble-philosopher-pointing-the-way look.

And the way was right at Hayley—gorgeous, wonderful, passionate Hayley.

"No," Justin said aloud.

"And he's down for the count," Ross said.

"What are they talking about?" Bryant asked Hayley.

"I don't know. Ignore them. Justin frequently spouts nonsense."

It wasn't fair. He was trying to do the right thing and they were ganging up on him.

Ross turned to Bryant. "I gather that you are a fan of the King?"

Bryant's eyes lit up and he launched into a gushing monologue. Ross encouraged him, thus keeping him occupied.

"I understand that Ross got a job on the *Mississippi Princess,*" Hayley said to Justin. She gingerly attempted to separate a rib from the slab on her plate.

Justin leapt through the conversational opening. "They were impressed with his singing at...the wedding," he finished uncomfortably.

Hayley glanced at him, then gave up on the ribs and ate her coleslaw. "Sounds like things are picking up for him."

"Yes."

The top Hayley wore looked like a leather version of the white wedding corset, except, when she moved, this one didn't.

Justin couldn't stand it, but he was going to have to. "I, uh, think I've finished with the revised valuations of your prize. The bridal fair has agreed to absorb some of the cost as advertisement. It should cut your tax bill in half."

"Oh, Justin, thank you!" Hayley's fork clattered to the table and she threw her arms around him.

Her thanks was overly exuberant. Justin didn't care. Feeling her in his arms again made his throat tighten. He squeezed his eyes shut so he could absorb as much from the moment as possible.

The moment didn't last nearly long enough. Hayley

released him when the waitress brought the rest of the food.

He opened his eyes and met Ross's amused ones. "Justin helped her with her taxes," Ross explained to Bryant.

"Does she need help with anything else?" Bryant asked. "I like the way she says thanks."

Ross laughed his hearty Shakespeare laugh.

Justin wanted to tackle Ross, then Bryant, then Ross again.

The rest of dinner followed a pattern of Ross encouraging Bryant's thoughts on Elvis Presley and making veiled comments designed to irritate Justin.

Hayley suddenly developed a thirst for Elvis trivia and made veiled comments designed to irritate Justin.

Justin was plenty irritated.

Dinner finally came to an end. Hayley had stood and Bryant was helping her on with her jacket. Justin was sitting on his hands.

"There she is. Your sweetheart in the arms of a friend." Ross hummed, then sang a few lines of "That's When Your Heartaches Begin." "It's amazing how the King's songs apply to so many of life's situations."

"Drop it, Ross," Justin warned.

He chuckled.

"Well, thanks very much," Hayley said to Bryant. "I enjoyed the evening."

"I'm going to follow you and see that you get home safely."

"That's not necessary," she said.

"Oh, yes, ma'am, it is."

Justin started to speak, but Ross stopped him. "This isn't your date."

And so Justin had to watch Hayley and Bryant leave the restaurant together. "I hope you're happy," he said to Ross.

Ross sat back and regarded Justin. "Moderately."

"You flung her into the arms of a sex-starved football coach!"

"What do you care?"

"I care!" Justin stared at the door as Hayley and Bryant disappeared from sight. "Did you see the way she was dressed?"

"Yes." Ross smiled, looking off into the distance. "Yes."

"Stop thinking about her."

"Have you been able to?"

Justin slumped in his chair.

"Justin," Ross said. "Admit it. Your grand master plan of future decadence and depravity is toast. And with my blessings."

BRYANT WALKED HAYLEY to her apartment door. He'd been sweet, but they hadn't clicked, at least not on her part. Not that she'd expected to. Still, she felt like kissing him good-night and goodbye.

"Good night, Bryant." She stood on her toes, intending to give him a quick kiss, when, incredibly, unbelievably, and quite stupidly on his part, she saw Justin peer out from the next hallway.

He'd *followed* her. He and Ross had ruined poor Bryant's dinner with her, and now Justin was spying on her.

That did it. She threw her arms around Bryant and planted the kiss of his dreams on him.

He was big, warm, burly, and not a bad kisser.

He was also a gentleman. Drawing back, he smiled at her. "Where is he?"

"Standing in the next hallway."

Bryant released her and grinned. "I saw his car pull in after me."

She looked ruefully at him. "I'm sorry."

"No." He shook his head. "You were a great date. Just what I needed to stop dragging around and start dating again, myself."

"I didn't intend to take advantage of you," she said. "But I love him and I can't help it."

"Man, do I hear that." Bryant heaved a great sigh.

They were two unhappy people, and it felt natural and comforting to hug him and be hugged in return.

And right now, Hayley needed comfort almost as much as she needed Justin.

10

THE KISS WAS BAD ENOUGH. Now what were they doing?

No longer trying to conceal his presence, Justin watched his former friend press Hayley's leather-clad body against his.

Something in him snapped.

He did not want Hayley pressing her body against another man and he did not want to press another woman's body against his. Just Hayley. For now and for all time, Justin wanted to be the only man entitled to hold her against him and kiss her and hear that little moan in the back of her throat.

As far as he was concerned, nothing else mattered.

He walked toward the embracing couple. "Hey, you two!" He tried for a hearty style that fooled no one. "Bryant, I thought you'd be long gone by now."

They pulled apart, but not completely, Justin noticed.

Bryant kept a protective arm around Hayley's shoulders. "Hello, there, Justin, ole buddy."

"Justin, what are you doing here?" Hayley's voice sounded flat and weary.

What *was* he doing here? "I—I—"

Pounding footsteps echoed in the concrete corridor.

"Justin, don't hit him!" Gasping and clutching his chest, Ross arrived on the scene. "She's not worth it. I beg you—stop this madness now!"

"You were going to *hit* him?" Hayley's jaw dropped.

"What do you mean 'She's not worth it'?" Justin stared at Ross—now also a former friend. "If I have to pound the living daylights out of him, she'd be worth it. She's worth *everything* to me!"

"Hang on, Justin. If you start throwing punches, you're only gonna hurt yourself," Bryant said, flexing a well-muscled arm for emphasis.

"Nobody is going to hit anybody until I hear more about being worth everything to him," Hayley said.

"That *was* a very interesting comment, Justin." Ross crossed his arms and stepped back. "Do feel free to elaborate."

"I'd kinda like to hear your intentions myself." Bryant crossed his arms, **as** well, but it had a more threatening effect.

"I—I—" Justin was trapped—trapped by a theatrical weasel and a former all-state linebacker.

Trapped by his feelings for the goddess in leather.

"I—I love her, damn it!" He glared at the men, then looked at Hayley. "I love you!"

She smiled her wide Hayley smile and cold settled in the pit of his stomach when he realized how close he'd come to losing her.

And then she was in his arms, where she belonged and where she was going to stay.

"And love triumphs at last," Ross murmured. "But how exhausting until it did."

"Hey, you know, you're pretty good," Bryant said.

"I am, aren't I?" Ross was obviously pleased with himself. "And I must compliment you on your excellent grasp of the situation and your keen improvisational abilities."

A chuckle rumbled deep within Bryant. "You don't take a team to the state finals three out of five years without learning how to size up a situation and make adjustments."

"Good point." Ross rubbed his hands together. "Well, our work here is done, but I'd like to hear more on the years after Elvis left the army, if you've got time."

"I always have time for the King," Bryant said.

They walked off together, snatches of "Can't Help Falling in Love" serenading Justin and Hayley.

"Did you hear that?" Justin murmured to her. They still stood outside Hayley's apartment, but he was afraid to let her out of his arms.

"Our song. You have wonderful friends."

"Including one who now has such a big head, his Elvis wig won't fit."

Hayley laughed, her body vibrating against him.

Justin kissed her.

"Um, Justin?" she asked, coming up for air. "What are we doing?"

Justin didn't even hesitate. "I've thrown my grand plan out the window and I'm improvising."

Her smile was even more luminous than usual.

He'd missed her smile. "Unlock the door. We have a wedding night to finish."

LOLA'S RAINBOW OF LOVE lecture hadn't covered "faux wedding night, part two."

By now, the rules were probably out the window anyway, Hayley thought.

She fumbled with the key because Justin was kissing her neck. She couldn't think because his hands were stroking her thighs. She didn't move because her door wouldn't unlock.

"Want me to kick it in?"

He meant it. She could hear the determination in his voice.

Fortunately the key turned and the door swung open.

Justin kicked it shut. "Take off your jacket."

His voice was harsh, his gaze hard and intent. Hayley hesitated. Was he angry?

"Please. You're so beautiful," he whispered.

Wonder stole over Hayley as she realized it was desire he felt, not anger. Desire for *her*. The intense desire of a man at the limit of his control. Desire not diluted by second thoughts or misgivings or regret. A desire that needed no more time to be sure.

She'd never seen undiluted desire before and hadn't recognized it. And now that she did, an answering desire unfurled within her.

He'd claimed her. He wanted her. Now.

And she wanted him.

Slowly she let her jacket fall off her shoulders and then to the floor.

Justin's gaze grew hotter and bluer.

"Shall I keep going?"

His lips parted, but he didn't say anything, so Hayley took that as a "yes."

The front lacing on the bustier was more decorative than functional, with a zipper up the back for convenience. Hayley wasn't after convenience at this particular moment.

Ever so slowly, she walked toward Justin, took his hand and put the end of the bow in his fingers. She stepped backward as he held the lacing and the bow came loose.

He dropped it as though it burned his fingers.

Hayley smiled to herself. He thought that was hot? Just wait until he touched *her*. She was steaming. Sizzling.

Through the metal grommets, she pulled first one lace, then the other, feeling the edges of the leather part.

Justin watched the movements of her fingers as though hypnotized.

When she got midway down, he licked his lips and swallowed, his nakedly longing gaze darting once to her face before helplessly following the inward and outward path of the laces.

What Hayley saw in his expression erased all the insidious doubts she'd had about her desirability since he'd left her. He wanted her so much, he could barely control himself. He was completely in her power and wasn't afraid to let her know it.

As a result, Hayley had never felt as supremely confident or as irresistible as she did at this moment.

Deliberately varying the rhythm she set, Hayley snapped one of the laces through the grommet.

Justin flinched, his hands balling into fists at his sides.

Hayley thrust out her chest to push the edges farther apart. The bustier wouldn't fall down until the waist was loosened.

All this tension made her long to stretch her muscles. Why not now? Straightening her shoulders, she moved her head from side to side, then back and around. Reaching high, she stretched, feeling her breasts pull out of the top of the bustier.

Justin made a sound she'd never heard a human being make before. In two steps he crossed the space between them and swept her into his arms.

In that moment, she realized that while her mother was chiffon and lace, Hayley was leather and skin. Not that chiffon didn't have its moments.

But this was a leather-and-skin moment, and Hayley reveled in the knowledge that she'd driven Justin insane with lust.

He carried her across her living room and into the bedroom.

Hayley was prepared to be flung onto the bed, but when Justin reached the bed, he stopped and stared at her.

"We have to talk," he said, letting her slide down the length of his body.

Hayley knew they had to talk, but she didn't want to talk *now*. "Later?"

He gave her a smile that liquefied her bones. "You'll be too tired to talk later."

She started unbuttoning his shirt. "Then talk fast."

"Hayley, I'm about to veer off a course I set for myself when I was fourteen, because I'm in love with you. I have to know if you feel the same way."

She looked at him in astonishment. "You know I love you. How could you even question it?"

"Because you've never said the words."

She tugged his shirttail out of his jeans. "I guess I've loved you for so long, I thought you knew."

"Yeah?" Justin had a huge smile on his face. "When did you know you loved me?"

"You really got my attention when you kissed me at the Peabody." Hayley worked his shirt off his shoulders. "But I think I was hooked when you ignored my sisters. No man has ever done that for me."

"Lucky for me."

"But I really knew I loved you when you said, 'Whatever was I thinking?' after one of my sisters mentioned our long engagement."

"I don't like long engagements," Justin said.

Hayley arched an eyebrow. "How do you know?"

"Because we're engaged now, and I don't like it."

"Are we engaged?"

"Aren't we?"

"You never said the words."

"We're getting married, aren't we?"

"Are those the words?"

"Hayley, nothing about our relationship has been by the books, so don't get technical on me now."

"*You* were technical. You wouldn't believe I loved you until I said the words."

He was quiet, then he spoke softly. "Actually, you haven't said the words."

"I have!"

"No, you said you loved me. You haven't said, 'I love you.'"

She rolled her eyes. "I love you."

"Thank you. Will you marry me?"

"You're welcome. Yes."

"Good. Now that all the technicalities have been satisfied..." Bending his head and using his teeth, he slowly finished unlacing the bustier.

By the time he finished, Hayley's mouth was dry and her heart was hammering.

The bustier fell open.

Justin drew a deep breath, his intent blue gaze roaming over her. "You are the perfect woman. Why didn't you wear a sign telling me so?"

"I thought you'd get the idea more from what I *wasn't* wearing." She tossed the bustier onto a chair.

"Good point." Justin then proceeded to set a new world's record for unpeeling leather from a woman.

"Why am I always naked and you're always dressed?" Hayley complained and looped her arms around his neck.

"Yet another good point." He kissed her, impressing her with his ability to undress at the same time.

"You have excellent hand-and-mouth coordination," she murmured. "A very useful talent in a man."

"Talent is nothing without practice," he murmured,

running his hands over her in long leisurely strokes. He bent to kiss her.

Hayley turned her head so his kiss landed on her jaw. "Just a minute. There are a few more tiny details to work out here. How exactly do I tell my mother I'm not Mrs. Sloane Devereaux?"

"You're asking *me* to think up something now?"

"I'm not the only one who'll be too tired later."

"Okay. I'll think of something." Justin nuzzled her neck.

"Are you thinking?"

"Hmm." He pressed close against her.

"You're thinking with the wrong part of your body."

"It has a mind of its own."

"Justin!"

"Okay, tell your mother that you broke up with Sloane before the wedding, and you were going to call everything off, but you met me. Since we hadn't known each other long, you were afraid she wouldn't approve, so you didn't tell her."

"Do you think she'll believe that?"

"It's the truth."

Hayley thought about it. It wasn't the entire truth, but it would be enough for her mother. She smiled. "You think well under pressure."

"Good. Stop talking so I can kiss you."

"Wait a minute. What about your plan? You know I have a huge tax bill and you still have Ross's loan to repay."

Justin's face turned serious. "I have more than that. You might want to wait awhile to get married."

"I don't want to wait. We both know we've got to pay off debts. We might as well be together while we do. I'm more worried about you feeling that you've missed something."

"I'll still experience everything, but now I'll experience it with you."

Hayley studied his face, seeing nothing but sincerity. "Are you sure?"

"Yes. Do you still have the gift basket?"

"By the bed. But one more thing."

Justin groaned.

"I want our wedding to be small, memorable and unweddinglike. Just us and the minister or judge."

"No," he said quietly.

Hayley's eyes widened, but he was serious. "Justin, I can't go through a production like that again."

"I'm not asking you to, but I am asking that my mother and stepfather be there. And probably Ross, too."

"Oh! Of course!" Hayley felt an overwhelming relief along with guilt. She'd been selfish about this wedding stuff.

Justin ran a hand along her thigh. "Anything else?"

"Yes," Hayley purred. "Get the gift basket."

_____Epilogue_____

"I THOUGHT YOUR NAME was Sloane." The Santa Claus judge from the *Mississippi Princess* studied the license Hayley and Justin had given him. They stood under the archway in the Viva Memphis! Wedding Chapel, which satisfied Hayley's criteria for memorable.

"That's his stage name," Ross explained.

"I see." The judge stuck the cigar back into his mouth and continued to study the license.

Justin's mother and stepfather exchanged looks. Of course the looks were nothing like the expressions on their faces when they saw the flying Elvis heads decorating the chapel walls.

To Hayley and Justin's relief, the judge didn't mention the recent date on the license, nor did he question their request to repeat the ceremony for the benefit of Justin's mother and stepfather.

"Everything *appears* to be in order." The slightest emphasis was the only acknowledgment he made of the unusual circumstances. He folded the paper and put it in his breast pocket. "Let's get started, then."

So they did.

The bride wore a simple white sheath and carried a bouquet of white roses.

The groom wore his new job-hunting suit.

The best man hummed a tasteful medley of Elvis Presley's greatest hits.

The groom's mother sobbed softly.

The judge pronounced them husband and wife.

And Hayley had the wedding of her dreams.

HARLEQUIN® *Temptation.*

It's a dating wasteland out there! So what's a girl to do when there's not a marriage-minded man in sight? Go hunting, of course.

Manhunting

Enjoy the hilarious antics of five intrepid heroines, determined to lead Mr. Right to the altar— whether he wants to go or not!

#669 *Manhunting in Memphis—* Heather MacAllister (February 1998)

#673 *Manhunting in Manhattan—* Carolyn Andrews (March 1998)

#677 *Manhunting in Montana—* Vicki Lewis Thompson (April 1998)

#681 *Manhunting in Miami—* Alyssa Dean (May 1998)

#685 *Manhunting in Mississippi—* Stephanie Bond (June 1998)

She's got a plan—to find herself a man!

Available wherever Harlequin books are sold.

THE MEN OF
BACHELOR CREEK

Alaska. A place where men could be men—and women were scarce!

To Tanner, Joe and Hawk, Alaska was the final frontier. They'd gone to the ends of the earth to flee the one thing they all feared—MATRIMONY. Little did they know that three intrepid heroines would brave the wilds to "save" them from their lonely bachelor existences.

Enjoy

**#662 CAUGHT UNDER
THE MISTLETOE!**
December 1997

#670 DODGING CUPID'S ARROW!
February 1998

#678 STRUCK BY SPRING FEVER!
April 1998

by Kate Hoffmann

Available wherever Harlequin books are sold.

HARLEQUIN® Temptation.

It's hot...
and it's out of control!

It's a two-alarm Blaze—
from one of Temptation's newest authors!

BLAZE

This spring, Temptation turns up the heat. Look for these bold, provocative, *ultra*-sexy books!

#679 PRIVATE PLEASURES
Janelle Denison
April 1998

Mariah Stevens wanted a husband. Grey Nichols
wanted a lover. But Mariah was determined.
For better or worse, there would be no more private
pleasures for Grey without a public ceremony.

#682 PRIVATE FANTASIES
Janelle Denison
May 1998

For Jade Stevens, Kyle was the man of her dreams. He
seemed to know her every desire—in bed and out. Little
did she know that he'd come across her book of private
fantasies—or that he intended to make every one come true!

BLAZE! **Red-hot reads from Temptation!**

HARLEQUIN®

Temptation.

KEY ♡ TO MY HEART

Unlock the secrets of romance just in time for the most romantic day of the year— Valentine's Day!

Key to My Heart
features three of your favorite authors,

Kasey Michaels,
Rebecca York
and Muriel Jensen,

to bring you wonderful tales of romance and Valentine's Day dreams come true.

As an added bonus you can receive Harlequin's special Valentine's Day necklace. FREE with the purchase of every *Key to My Heart* collection.

Available in January,
wherever Harlequin books are sold.

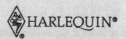

HARLEQUIN®

PHKEY349

DEBBIE MACOMBER

invites you to the

HEART OF TEXAS

Join Debbie Macomber as she brings you the lives
and loves of the folks in the ranching community
of Promise, Texas.

If you loved Midnight Sons—don't miss
Heart of Texas! A brand-new six-book series
from Debbie Macomber.

Available in February 1998
at your favorite retail store.

Heart of Texas by Debbie Macomber

Lonesome Cowboy	February '98
Texas Two-Step	March '98
Caroline's Child	April '98
Dr. Texas	May '98
Nell's Cowboy	June '98
Lone Star Baby	July '98

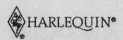

HARLEQUIN®

HPHRT1